D1435565

A JACK CHRISTIE ADVENTURE

DAY OF DELIVERANCE

JOHNNY O'BRIEN

templar books
an imprint of Candlewick Press

Text copyright © 2010 by Johnny O'Brien
Illustrations copyright © 2010 by Nick Spender

First U.S. edition 2010

Library of Congress Cataloging-in-Publication Data

O'Brien, Johnny.
Day of deliverance / Johnny O'Brien. —1st U.S. ed.
p.   cm.—(A Jack Christie Adventure ; 2)
Summary: To thwart their archenemy, Pendelshape, and his misguided notion of changing history, schoolboy Jack Christie and his friend Angus travel back in time to foil a plot to assassinate Elizabeth I, meeting playwright Christopher Marlowe and a young actor named William Shakespeare along the way.
ISBN 978-0-7636-5075-9
[1. Time travel—Fiction. 2. Adventure and adventurers—Fiction.
3. Elizabeth, I, Queen of England 1533–1603—Fiction.
4. Great Britain—History—Elizabeth, 1558–1603—Fiction.
5. Adventure and adventurers—Fiction. 6. Science fiction.]   I. Title. II. Series.
PZ7.O1272Das 2010
[Fic]—dc22   2010010710

10 11 12 13 14 15 LBM 10 9 8 7 6 5 4 3 2 1

Printed in Melrose Park, IL, U.S.A.

This book was typeset in Berkeley Book.

TEMPLAR BOOKS
an imprint of
Candlewick Press
99 Dover Street
Somerville, Massachusetts 02144

www.candlewick.com

For Sally, Tom, Peter, and Anna

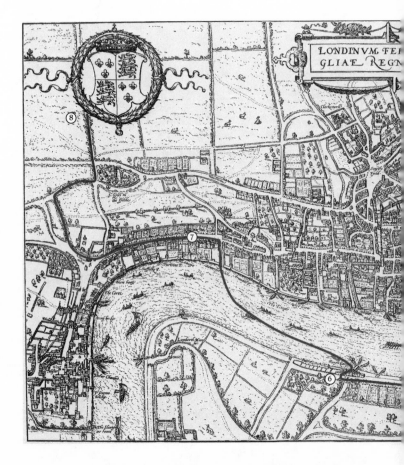

JACK'S FIRST TRIP

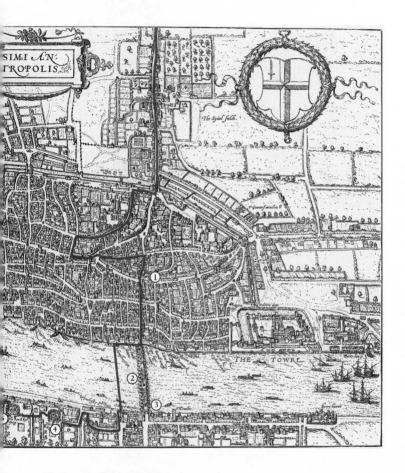

TO LONDON

Contents

Prologue

It has been six months since Jack and Angus made the mind-boggling discovery that their school, Soonhope High, is a front for a secret team of scientists who control the most powerful technology ever conceived by man—the technology of time travel. At the heart of the technology is a machine called the Taurus. Jack's dad, Professor Christie, was part of the team who originally designed the Taurus. But there was a huge disagreement between him and the other scientists. Jack's dad wants to use the technology to make changes in the past which he thinks will make things better—like stopping wars. He has attracted some passionate and brilliant supporters, including Dr. Pendelshape, who until last year was Jack's history teacher. Pendelshape and Christie, together with their small band of followers, who call themselves the Revisionists, developed very sophisticated computer simulations to model interventions in the past that could benefit mankind. Their ideas clash with the other scientists, their former colleagues, who believe that changing things in the past, however well-intentioned, is dangerous and could have unforeseen consequences. These scientists tried to do away with Christie, who escaped into exile—leaving Jack and his mom, Carole, behind when Jack was only six years old. With Professor Christie gone, the scientists formed a group called VIGIL to ensure that the time travel technology was kept secret—but still in working order, should it ever be needed.

Jack and Angus became embroiled when, unknown to VIGIL, Professor Christie created a second Taurus while in exile and proceeded to try to stop the assassination of Archduke Ferdinand in Sarajevo in June 1914—the event that triggered the First World War. Professor Christie was being secretly helped by Dr. Pendelshape, who VIGIL believed to be loyal and who remained at Soonhope High. Jack and

Day of Deliverance

Angus found themselves pawns in a battle between the two camps. Jack's loyalties were torn. In the end, having witnessed the dangers of time travel and intervening in the past firsthand, both Jack and Angus decided that the right course of action was to side with VIGIL.

So both sides are at an impasse. VIGIL can't find Christie, Pendelshape, and the second Taurus. And Professor Christie, for his part, won't use his Taurus while Jack—his son—is under the guard of VIGIL for fear that VIGIL might harm Jack in retribution. But Christie is unaware that increasingly Jack's and Carole's loyalties are with VIGIL. The atmosphere at VIGIL is tense. Although their security is highly sophisticated, they are worried about what the Revisionists' next move may be.

A Poisoned Sword

Jack thrust the rapier forward. Angus jumped back, but this time he was not quick enough. The blade pierced his flesh, and an ominous red patch appeared on his white shirt. Angus glanced down at the wound and looked back at his opponent with an expression of rage on his face. A frisson of excitement rippled through the crowd. The contest was proving better than they could have possibly wished. Jack was exhilarated—a final blow and it would all be over.

But his confidence was short-lived. The strike had found its mark but had also unbalanced him momentarily, and Angus came back with a violent counterthrust. His blade flashed through the air and caught Jack in the ribs. There was a gasp from the crowd. The foil was so sharp that Jack scarcely felt it. But in only a few seconds his own blade felt much heavier in his hand, and his breathing quickened. Sensing his chance, Angus darted forward once more, his sword aimed at Jack's chest. This time Jack spotted the move and swayed to one side. Angus's forward momentum presented Jack with an opportunity. He grabbed his opponent by the arm and heaved him onward while simultaneously thrusting out his leg. Angus tripped over Jack's extended leg and spun through the air, landing with a crunching thud, his sword spinning from his hand. Jack pounced on him and they became locked in a deadly struggle. But he should have known better than to take on Angus in a wrestling match. Angus was much stronger and soon had Jack pinned on his back beneath him. Angus grasped Jack's sword hand and banged it hard on the ground until Jack relinquished his grip. Angus lowered his face toward Jack's and sneered.

"You will die."

Day of Deliverance

Jack was nailed to the ground. He was wounded, and he had no weapon. Angus's massive bulk was pressing down on him. But it wasn't over yet. He gritted his teeth and with a superhuman effort jerked his knee upward into Angus's crotch. Angus wailed in pain, and Jack seized the moment to wriggle free. He snatched up a sword and wheeled around. The sword felt different—heavier and unbalanced—but it didn't matter now. Angus jumped back to his feet and grabbed the other sword, and the two of them circled each other, panting like wounded animals. The crowd jeered. Jack's remaining energy was melting away—he knew he only had seconds left. There was blood all over the floor and Angus slipped. He was only distracted for a moment, but it was enough. Jack leaped forward to land a second, and this time fatal, blow. Angus screamed as blood from a second wound spurted from his chest. He dropped to one knee and looked up at Jack with an unexpected expression—almost apologetic.

"The poison . . . I have been killed by my own treachery," he stammered.

Jack glanced down at the sword that dangled loosely from his hand—and suddenly he understood. He had snatched up Angus's sword, which must have been dipped in poison before the contest. Jack had already been injured with the same sword, which meant that in less than a minute, both of them would be dead.

But there was still time to see to unfinished business. Jack knew what he had to do.

Clutching his chest to stem the bleeding, he staggered across to where his uncle sat cowering behind the long banqueting table. The food and drink was laid out—still untouched. Jack mounted the table and fixed his eyes menacingly on his uncle, who sank back into his chair, shaking. There was to be no mercy, and Jack did not hesitate. He thrust the sword into his uncle's heart.

Words, Words, Words

Miss Beattie scurried onto the stage. "Well done, everyone! Lights!"

There was a spontaneous round of applause from the cast and crew. Nothing was being left to chance. The week before, Miss Beattie had even arranged for a special fight choreographer to come in and help them with the sword fight between Hamlet and Laertes in the last scene. It was all perfectly safe, of course, and the flashing swords reassuringly blunt, but there was always tension in the air during the famous scene, and everyone stopped what they were doing to watch. And today, with Angus a reluctant and unrehearsed stand-in for Laertes (who was sick), who knows what might have happened.

"That's all coming together quite well." Miss Beattie was pleased with the progress. "Only two weeks to go now. . . ."

Jack looked down at Tommy McGough from his position still perched upon the table. Tommy was playing Claudius, Hamlet's uncle, and he nervously opened one eye.

"Did I survive?"

"Looks like it," Jack said. "Don't know how you get away with it. Every rehearsal I somehow manage to miss."

"Dangerous business, this Shakespeare stuff . . ."

Angus bounded over from center stage, flushed with excitement from the sword fight with Jack.

"That was awesome."

"Told you."

Miss Beattie removed the pouch of stage blood from under Angus's shirt, which was almost completely red.

Day of Deliverance

"What a mess," the English teacher fussed.

Angus grinned. "I thought I would go for Hamlet-meets-Terminator. . . . Everyone likes a bit of blood, don't they?"

Without looking up, she replied, "Actually, you're right. When they did these plays in the old days they wouldn't have skimped on the blood . . . used goat's blood, probably. The audiences loved gore. There's even a story of actors using a real musket in one production. It went off, and someone in the audience got his head blown off by mistake."

Miss Beattie was always saying stuff like this. It was one reason why drama was popular at their school—and successful. The whole town of Soonhope would likely turn up for the end-of-term performances of *Hamlet*.

"Is that true, Miss Beattie?"

"Apparently. They just dragged the body out. The next day, they were on again. They weren't too concerned about gun control in the sixteenth century, but I doubt they used the musket."

"I could get into that," Angus said.

Jack elbowed him. "See—I told you it was worth coming."

"Well—the fighting was good fun, but I couldn't stand Shakespeare for too long—you know, all those . . . words."

Miss Beattie looked up at Angus with a steely eye. Her good humor evaporated and a shadow passed over her face. Although at nearly six feet Angus towered over her, it was as if he physically shrank by a good six inches when he saw her expression.

"You've done it now . . ." Jack murmured and glanced sidelong at Tommy, who returned the look, grimacing.

"Words!" Miss Beattie rolled the *r* in her strong Scottish brogue. "WORRRDS!" She yelled again louder—and it came from her lips like a dart from a blowpipe. "Is that all you have to say on the matter—WORRRDS?"

Everyone around the stage stopped what they were doing and turned toward them. Miss Beattie, for all her boundless enthusiasm, was also prone to dramatic changes in mood. As a result, Angus was about to receive what was popularly termed by the pupils of Soonhope High School as a Beattie Beating. It was never pleasant.

"But, Miss . . ." Angus bravely tried to stand his ground, but it was too late. It was if he had inadvertently triggered a small thermonuclear device.

"I'll tell you this—laddie—not any old words . . . nearly one million words in forty plays and more than one hundred and fifty four sonnets and poems . . . and not just any old plays and sonnets, but the most sublime writing the world has ever read—even after four hundred years. Words? Shakespeare invented them. Lots of them: *critical, frugal, dwindle, extract, zany, leapfrog, vast, hereditary, excellent, eventful, lonely* . . . and phrases, new phrases like: *vanish into thin air, brave new world, fool's paradise, sea change, sorry sight, in a pickle, budge an inch, cold comfort, flesh and blood, foul play, bated breath, cruel to be kind, fair play, green-eyed monster* . . ." She paused only to take a deep breath. Then she was off again. "These are WORDS and phrases that have been used so much, they have become clichés. . . . They are words and phrases that I use—God help us—even *you* use— Shakespeare was the world's greatest writer and helped define the world's richest language—the English language—*your* language— and so gave us the very tools to think and feel. He gave us the *essence of humanity.* Do you get it? Do you understand? So please don't talk to me about WORRRDS!"

There was stunned silence around the stage as everyone wondered if there might be more—whether this was to be a tactical nuclear strike—or the full-blown strategic version that would take out the whole of Soonhope. Thankfully, the color in Miss Beattie's cheeks normalized from a deep purple to its more usual pink hue. Nevertheless, Angus continued to stare at a spot on the end of one of his shoes for a full ten seconds before he finally mumbled, "Yes, Miss. Sorry, Miss."

Miss Beattie gave a final sigh of indignation and said, "That's all right, Mr. Jud." She looked around and clapped her hands. "Now everyone—let's get this cleaned up—it's almost four o'clock."

But something that Miss Beattie had said stuck in Jack's mind and as he and Tommy put away the props, his curiosity overcame his fear.

"Sorry, Miss—did you say a *million* words? I mean, written by one man—Shakespeare?"

The auburn-haired Queen Elizabeth I
in "The Armada Portrait"

"Yes, Jack, I think that's about right."

"But it just sounds like an awful lot for one man to do . . ."

"It is. There are lots of theories—generally rubbish—that he did not actually write his material, but that others did. Shakespeare lived during the English Renaissance—it was a boom time for plays and playwrights and art and artists generally. More than fifty candidates have been suggested as the 'real' Shakespeare—people like Christopher Marlowe."

"Who?"

Miss Beattie was overseeing the flow of props back into the cupboard, "No, Tommy, put the swords *properly* into the sword cart, or they'll get damaged." She looked back at Jack. "Sorry, Jack—what was that?"

"Marlowe—was he like Shakespeare, then?"

"He influenced Shakespeare, but he died before Shakespeare really got going, in 1593, I think, when he was only twenty-nine. He was murdered. He was a spy."

"A writer and a spy?"

"Yes, maybe even a double agent. I know it sounds odd, but there were quite a few writers that were, at the time. They often studied at Oxford or Cambridge—although actually Shakespeare didn't—and the universities were hotbeds of radicalism."

"What do you mean?"

She sighed. "You're insatiable, Jack." She turned to lock the cupboard and then looked at him sympathetically. "Look—we don't really have time to go into the whole of sixteenth-century politics right now . . . but for our next lesson—maybe we'll do it in more detail." She thought for a minute. "Tell you what, come over here . . ." She scurried over to her things at the side of the stage and pulled out a large book.

"There you go, that should get you started." She handed the tome over to Jack. It was entitled, simply, *Elizabeth I*. On the front there was the famous Armada portrait of the auburn-haired queen in an elaborately decorated dress covered in jewels, with one hand draped over a globe and pointing to Virginia, England's first colony in the New

World. Behind the queen, the Spanish Armada could be seen—sailing to its doom.

"Knowing you, Jack, you should be able to finish that off in a couple of hours. It's all there. And it's not just about Shakespeare and Marlowe, you know. It was a period of deep religious conflict between Catholics and Protestants—a struggle for the very soul of man. And this religious conflict was intertwined with the political struggles between countries. Spain was the global superpower but when England defeated the Spanish Armada, that all started to change. If it hadn't been for that, we might be living in a Catholic country today and speaking Spanish—and so might most of the world. We would probably be having tapas for school dinners." Miss Beattie stopped. "There I go again . . . prattling away . . ." She tapped the book. "Anyway, I'll leave it with you."

Jack leafed through the book.

"Who's that?" He pointed to a picture of a confident young man in flashy Elizabethan clothes.

"That's the man—Marlowe—only portrait of him—only twenty-one and dressed up to the nines."

"What does that mean?" Jack pointed to some Latin words on top of the picture.

Miss Beattie laughed. "'What feeds me destroys me'—apparently. Just about sums Marlowe up—he was, how shall I put it, on the edge."

Jack didn't really understand what the words meant, but was already leafing through the rest of the book. There were pictures of ships: great Spanish galleons stuffed with treasure from the New World, terrifying fire ships let loose by the English on the anchored Spanish fleet off Calais, the de-masted *Revenge* in the Azores, where, in a fit of macho bravado, Sir Richard Grenville took on twelve great Spanish galleons alone—only to die. There were extraordinarily beautiful buildings, soaring edifices of glass and stone—a far cry from the brutal castles of the Middle Ages. Then there were the people: kings and queens, princes, players, and poets. As Jack leafed through the volume, he noticed a small illustration on the bottom of one of the pages. The caption read: *Elizabethan Troupe*. It was a color plate of a

Christopher Marlowe
"What feeds me destroys me."

group of actors in various costumes. There was one dressed as a court jester and next to him, in stark contrast, another dressed as a priest, or more like a monk. There was a third who looked slightly more important—a country gentleman with a fine cloak and a neat, pointed beard.

"Head in a book again?" Angus leaned over Jack's shoulder. It looked like everyone else had left. "Do you want to get something at Gino's?"

Jack snapped the book shut.

"Why not?" He stuffed the book in his bag.

"Well, stop reading and let's go!"

Gino's

Jack sat behind Angus on his motorbike. He was nervous. Usually trips on the back of Angus's bike did not go well. Angus was seventeen now and had his license. His old two-stroke Husqvarna had been left at his family's place up in Rachan, and he had taken to riding one of the farm's more powerful four-stroke Yamaha 250Fs. When he could afford the gas he took it to school—avoiding the one-hour bus journey that picked its way painfully through Soonhope Valley.

Angus turned back the throttle and the engine wailed; he dropped the clutch and they set off. Thankfully, Angus avoided the obligatory wheelie, which he usually performed just to frighten Jack. Soon they reached the bridge over the river, which was quite low from a dry spell. The big Presbyterian church at the head of High Street loomed ahead of them, and Jack remembered what Miss Beattie had been saying about the "struggle for men's souls." Even in Soonhope, with less than two thousand inhabitants, he knew of at least five churches, all of different denominations. It occurred to Jack that he hadn't actually been inside any of them, and he wasn't sure how many of the local population had either.

High Street was busy but Angus managed to squeeze the bike right in front of Gino's, and as they went in, the welcoming smell of coffee and ice cream wafted over them. Gino was manning the espresso machine while Francesca, his daughter, polished glasses grumpily. Gino was as jolly as ever.

"What can I get you?"

"Hi, Gino." Angus looked up at the endless menu of drinks and snacks above the counter. But he already knew what he wanted. "I'll have the double Gino-chino, extra shot, full fat, with caramel and extra whipped cream . . . and don't forget the cherry." He looked over at

Francesca and winked provocatively, adding in a deep voice, "Shaken . . . not stirred." Francesca rolled her eyes and tutted loudly.

"You have no chance there. Turinelli family outta your league, son."

Angus shrugged. "Oh well—just give me four grilled cheeses."

"Cutting back?" Jack asked.

"Not exactly. We're playing Melrose tomorrow—last game of the season. If we win—we win the league. Need to bulk up."

"And Jack, my friend, what are you having?"

"Thanks, Gino; what the hell, I'll go for a Gino-chino as well—but without the bells and whistles, and make it just one grilled cheese . . . but don't tell Mom."

"It's coming. . . . Take a seat, boys."

Gino had recently tried to convert his popular Italian bistro into a greasy spoon diner—he had even gotten himself a jukebox (which didn't work). It had been a brave attempt, but somehow it all looked a bit out of place on High Street of traditional Soonhope. Jack and Angus settled into one of the booths and soon, in hushed tones, they were discussing their favorite subject.

"Do you think we did the right thing?"

It was Angus's favorite question, and Jack replied with his usual answer.

"Yes—we did the right thing. I'm sure of it. The computer simulations that Dad and Pendelshape created to model the changes they wanted to make in history were good, sure, but you could never be certain that by going back in time you might not do something that would have unforeseen consequences for the future. That's the risk. That's the whole reason that VIGIL was set up. And that's why we sided with them in the end."

"I guess. It's too bad, though."

"Why?"

"Well, I know going back to 1914 . . . well, it was dangerous and stuff, and a lot of bad things happened . . ."

"Yes, Angus," Jack said slowly, making sure the point sank in, "that's why nobody wants to do it again. Time travel, and especially using the Taurus to make changes to history . . . It's a bad idea.

Remember your Great-Grandfather Ludwig in the trenches? If that bayonet had been a few inches to the right, he may have died, and you wouldn't be here."

"I know, but"—Angus grinned—"you've got to admit, it was pretty exciting."

Jack shook his head. "Sometimes I wonder about you. We can say that sitting here now. But it didn't feel like that to me at the time. We were lucky to get away with our lives. Meddling in time should be avoided. VIGIL and their leaders—the Rector, Counselor Inchquin, all of them—they're trying to do the right thing. Dad and Pendelshape, the Revisionists, for all their brains and good intentions, are just plain wrong. We're on the side of VIGIL now."

Angus shrugged.

Gino ambled over to their booth. "Two Gino-chinos, one grilled cheese for you and . . . four for you."

"Great, Gino. Thanks a lot."

Jack looked at Angus's plate. "You're not seriously going to eat all that, are you?"

"I don't really want to. I'm doing it more out of a sense of duty to the team," Angus replied regretfully—as if he were making some terrible sacrifice. He opened one of the sandwiches and poured salt, vinegar, and ketchup onto the cheese inside before quickly resealing the bread. He then took a large bite, and the contents leaked out from each side.

"Gross."

"Actually, very tasty," Angus replied, his mouth full. It didn't stop him from continuing their conversation.

"But what about your dad? Don't you feel bad about him? If VIGIL ever gets hold of him, they'll kill him for sure."

Angus was never one for subtlety, and Jack grimaced. "Thanks for reminding me." There was an awkward silence, and then Jack shrugged. "I try not to think about it." He swallowed. "And I don't know, maybe one day there will be a way . . . a way that VIGIL and Dad can be reconciled." He looked down at his plate. "Maybe then Mom and Dad could even get back together."

Angus swallowed and took a swig of his Gino-chino. "Sorry, Jackster—didn't mean to"—he shrugged—"Well, you know."

"It's all right. Anyway, we're fully signed-up members of VIGIL now. Don't forget what that means."

Angus wiped his mouth, and his eyes lit up. "How could I forget?"

Jack remembered the VIGIL inauguration ceremony that he and Angus had participated in after they had returned from Sarajevo. As things settled down, they learned that VIGIL's role was not only to be ready to counteract any attempts by the Revisionists to meddle in history, but also to identify and train promising students and enroll them in VIGIL. This was one reason for secreting the Taurus complex and VIGIL headquarters in an ordinary school: it was easy to identify potential candidates. In this way, VIGIL would ensure the continuation of the VIGIL cause from one generation to the next and ensure the future safety of mankind. This was critical, particularly while the Revisionist threat was still alive. Jack's and Angus's experiences in 1914 had made them instant VIGIL veterans and obvious candidates for enrollment.

Jack's cell phone went off and he pulled it from his pocket. "Text from Mom probably—wondering where I am . . ."

Angus returned to his second sandwich.

Jack peered at the screen. "Don't recognize that number . . ." He read the message. "Funny." Jack's brow furrowed. "What do you think of this?"

"Of what?"

Jack read the text aloud: "'Jack, meet at old lookout. Very urgent. Come now.' What can that mean?"

"You've got an admirer—finally."

"Funny."

"The old lookout—that's the fire tower, isn't it; you know, top of Glentress? We used to go up there on the bike."

"Yeah, but who's this from? There's no name . . ."

Angus grinned mischievously. "Only one way to find out."

"But I can't do that without alerting VIGIL. I've got this stupid tracker on my ankle, remember?" Jack pulled up one leg of his pants a little to show Angus the discreet wireless tracker that ensured his whereabouts were always known to VIGIL. Jack was a valuable asset to VIGIL—and the tracker was just one of the ways they made sure he was properly protected. Most of the time he forgot about it, but sometimes it made him frustrated and even angry that he had been put in this position.

"Oh yeah, I forgot about that." Angus thought for a moment, and then a twinkle came to his eye. "On the other hand, you could just say you temporarily forgot about it or something. Might be a laugh to see how quickly they send in air support when they know you've gone AWOL. It's good to keep them on their toes."

Jack was not sure. "I don't know, Angus . . ."

"Come on, Jack, who dares wins and all that . . ." He nodded at Jack's sandwich, "Finish that." He stood up. "And let's go find out who your mystery girlfriend is."

The Tower

In a moment they were back on Angus's bike heading out of town toward the forest. The forestry commission owned large tracts of land above Soonhope and had populated it with a pine and spruce monoculture that spread for many square miles across the hills. Soon they were powering up one of the forest paths, a plume of dust rising from the back tire. At intervals there were fire warning signs with a picture of a red flame and lists of DON'TS beneath. Don't do this, and don't do that. It was as if they had been put there by VIGIL. But you needed more than signs to deter Angus. He worked his way up and down the gears as they ascended steadily. At one point the forest path swept around to the right, and a steeper path rose through the thick woodlands at an angle from the bend.

Angus pulled up and shouted through his helmet. "Hold on—I'm going to take a shortcut."

Before Jack had time to object, Angus shot the bike up the narrow path. All Jack could do was hang on. After a while, the steep path leveled off and they picked up speed. The densely packed conifers whizzed past on both sides.

Suddenly, a shape appeared in front of them—right in the middle of the path. It was a man, just standing there, looking at the oncoming bike as if caught in a trance. Angus hit the front brake and then the rear a split second later. He twisted the handlebars to avoid the man, and as he did so, both tires lost their grip on the loose surface. In a split second, the bike, Jack, and Angus were horizontal and sliding along the ground. The man leaped free moments before impact, and the boys slid to a halt in the tall grass beside the path. Jack's heart was pounding, and his leg hurt from where the bike had pressed down on it as they had scraped along the path. Thankfully nothing seemed to be broken. Angus was first to his feet.

"What the . . . ?"

Jack groaned and pulled himself into a seated position—and immediately wished he hadn't. He felt nauseous.

The man looked at them—they had slid past him by a good fifty feet. He was maybe midforties, slim, and fit-looking, and wore jeans and hiking boots and a gray fleece jacket. He had not shaved for a few days, and his blond hair was ruffled.

"What the hell are you doing? Are you trying to get us all killed?" Angus bellowed.

The man did not reply. It was as if he was weighing something in his mind. Then, saying nothing, he turned and melted back into the thick, dark woods.

Angus was apoplectic. "What? He just ran off!"

Jack pulled himself to his feet, dusting himself down. He could see scrapes on his leg through the rips in his jeans.

"Are you OK?" Angus said. "I can't believe that guy!"

"We probably shouldn't be on this path, anyway." Jack looked down at the bike, still lying on its side. "Will it start?"

Angus hauled the machine up, inspecting the scrapes to the gas tank and chrome.

"What a mess. If I ever see that guy again . . ."

He straddled the bike and tried the engine. It fired immediately.

"Thank God for that."

"What now?"

"Well, we might as well finish what we came up to do." Angus looked at Jack's pale face. "If you're still up for it."

"I'll survive." Jack mounted the passenger seat gingerly, and Angus set off—this time at a more sedate pace.

After a while, they left the dark green canopy, and were released above the tree line, where they rejoined the main forest path. Apart from the mystery hill-walker they had nearly hit on the way up, there was no one around. The fire lookout tower loomed into view as they crested a final ridge.

Angus cut the engine and the air became still. They took off their helmets and walked toward the tower. Jack moved with a slight limp, but Angus seemed to show no effects of falling off the bike. Sometimes it was like he was indestructible.

"Doesn't seem to be anyone here at all. No sign of your mystery admirer."

Jack shrugged. "Weird. Shall we go up?"

"Why not?"

They clambered up the wooden ladder to the lookout cabin.

Angus knocked on the rough wooden door. "Hello! Anyone home?"

There was silence, except for a light spring breeze which teased the top of the trees in the distance.

"Nothing—come on, let's check it out."

The door opened into a crude wooden room, which gave panoramic views of the surrounding forest and hills. It was like being in a small boat in a big green ocean. Far below you could see the river meandering its way down the valley, shining like a silver ribbon in the late afternoon sun. In the middle of the cabin was a three-dimensional model—it was pretty rough; a sort of topographical map of the entire surrounding area. It showed the nearby hills, paths, streams, river, peaks, villages, and the position of the other fire towers laid out in detail across three square feet of plastic and modeling paint. From this lofty position, you could see how the fire wardens would have a sense of control—of watchful power.

"Nothing here. Certainly no clue as to your mystery texter . . ."

Jack peeped into the one adjoining room. It was a bedroom—but more the size of a large cupboard.

"Hey, looks like there's been someone sleeping here."

In the room, there was a sleeping bag, a gas burner, and a couple of books.

"One of the wardens?"

"Early in the year for them."

"And I'm not sure they'd be reading these."

Jack picked up a couple of books that had been left behind. One was entitled *Principles of Quantum Mechanics*. It looked old and was by someone named Paul Dirac. The other book was the complete works of William Shakespeare. It was open at one page, and the reader had circled an extract in pencil. Jack peered down at the book.

"That's funny—this guy's been reading *Hamlet*."

"Please, no, I've had enough of *Hamlet* for one day." Angus looked around furtively. "Beattie's probably got this place wired, just to check that I don't say anything critical."

Jack read the circled lines:

Let us go in together,
And still your fingers on your lips, I pray.
The time is out of joint—O cursèd spite,
That ever I was born to set it right!
Nay, come, let's go together.

"Sorry, Jackster, that sounds like complete gobbledygook—as per usual."

Jack smiled. "It's actually one of my lines from *Hamlet*."

"I suppose you're going to tell me what it means and make yourself feel clever."

"Of course. From what I remember of what Beattie said, Hamlet's basically saying that things in Denmark, which he calls 'the time,' are all messed up because of what his uncle, King Claudius, has done—killing Hamlet's father and marrying his mother. Hamlet's thinking about what he has to do to make it right . . . and he's kind of worried and also resentful that he's the one who has to sort it out. Do you understand?"

"No."

Jack rolled his eyes.

"All I can say is it's a bit weird that someone's up here, and maybe we shouldn't hang around too long. He or she might come back. I don't want to bump into some hobo who reads Shakespeare and does math for fun."

"So who sent the text? Do you think it was whoever's been hanging out here?"

"It's all creepy. I think we should go."

They turned to leave. As they did so, they noticed an envelope pinned to the inside of the wooden cabin door. Jack's heart leaped when he saw what was written on it. It was in scrawled script and read simply:

JACK CHRISTIE.

Jack pulled the envelope down and ripped it open. Inside was a letter.

Jack,

I hoped that I would finally be able to see you in person again and that we would have time to talk. However, I fear that VIGIL may soon learn of my location, and therefore I have left in haste. This is a sad time for me. As you already know, I have been exiled from my former colleagues in VIGIL and as a result have not seen you or Carole for nine years. This is a cause of great sorrow. But now, I also find myself in disagreement with my friend Pendelshape and the Revisionist team, which I set up in opposition to VIGIL.

Some months ago we started work on a new timeline simulation—one that aims to bring about great good for humanity. However, I could not accept further development of this simulation before I knew that you could be safely isolated from VIGIL and brought over to our side. Pendelshape and my Revisionist colleagues have become frustrated by my attitude, to say the least. We have argued and now, fearing their retribution, I have left them. Furthermore, with your safety in mind, I have, as of today, taken the unprecedented step of warning VIGIL of what I know of Pendelshape's plans. I now find myself alone in the world—a complete fugitive.

I never wanted to put you in this position or for you to

have experienced what you already have. However, I live in
hope that we can one day meet and that you will join me in
my mission.

—Dad

Jack stared at the letter in stunned silence. It all came together—
the strange books in the tower . . . the man on the path . . .

"Your dad . . . he's been *here*?" Angus said incredulously.

"Yeah. And I think that was the guy we nearly ran down. I thought
I sort of vaguely recognized him. He was running away."

"From what?"

"From just about everyone, I guess."

Suddenly, from away in the distance, they heard a faint mechanical
whirring. Jack and Angus peered out the front of the fire tower toward
the direction of the noise.

". . . and probably from that thing."

The whirring rapidly crescendoed into a pounding *whup, whup,
whup* as below them a large helicopter skimmed the top of the trees
and headed up toward the fire tower. In seconds the helicopter was
hovering right above them. The noise was deafening, and the whole
wooden structure of the tower shook on its foundations. The pilot
circled once, and then the aircraft descended, the thrashing rotor
blades throwing up a maelstrom of dust and debris. Finally it touched
down on a flat patch of ground near the tower, and the pilot cut the
engine. Jack and Angus opened the door of the cabin. In the distance,
they could see a convoy of three Land Rovers approaching along the
forest path. As the noise from the helicopter engine subsided and the
Land Rovers pulled up near the tower, Jack could hear loud barking
from the backs of the vehicles. Dogs.

Pendelshape Panic

Two figures stepped from the helicopter. They crouched low to avoid the rotor blades, which were still spinning at a dizzying speed. One was a tall man in his forties, with fine features and a head of silver hair. He had an air of distinction and authority about him. It was Counselor Inchquin. He was the chairman of VIGIL and oversaw all its operations. Next to him was another tall figure—slimmer than Inchquin with a bald head. By day he was Soonhope High's headmaster—the Rector—and he was still wearing his trademark black gown. The Rector was VIGIL's second-in-command.

Mr. Belstaff and Mr. Johnstone stepped from the first Land Rover. They were the gym teachers from the school, but they also formed part of VIGIL's security and response team. All members of VIGIL had day jobs which belied their second life as key members of the VIGIL network. All four men converged on Jack and Angus, who stood nervously at the bottom of the fire tower.

"Is he in there?" the Rector asked, a mixture of concern and aggression in his voice.

"He's gone," Jack replied.

"Damn," Inchquin hissed. "No sign at all?"

"He left this letter." Jack handed the letter they had found inside to the Rector, who scanned it quickly.

"Well, it confirms the message we received earlier," the Rector said. "You saw nothing else, boys?"

Jack was torn. The dogs cooped up in the Land Rovers were in a frenzy. Was Jack really going to admit that they had nearly run down someone who they thought to be his father—only for VIGIL to release a pack of hounds on him in some brutal manhunt?

Clearly the thought had not even crossed Angus's mind. "We think we might have seen him." He nodded down the hill. "But I don't think you'll find him now."

Inchquin looked at Jack sympathetically. "Sorry, Jack—we have to try. He's too important to just let go." He turned toward Belstaff and Johnstone. "Take the men and the dogs—see if you can track him down. He may not have gotten far. Hurry."

"What's going on, sir? How did you know he would be here?" Jack said. "And . . . what does the letter from Dad *mean*?"

"We intercepted your phone message. And then the tracker alarm indicated you were exiting the Soonhope safe zone. Sorry, Jack, you know we can't take any chances." The Rector waved the letter in the air. "And this letter basically means trouble. We will explain back at HQ." He nodded at the helicopter. "You need to come with us. We have very little time."

"What about my bike?" Angus said.

"The men will take care of it. I can assure you we have much more important business. Now, let's go."

The sun was low in the sky as Angus and Jack peered from the helicopter as it swooped in above Soonhope High's extensive athletic fields. They had a bird's-eye view of the austere Victorian main school building, which sat in secluded grounds some ways out of the town. Until ten years ago it had been empty. Then it had been redeveloped by an endowment from a charitable trust, which they now knew had been a front for VIGIL. Since it had been bought, the building had spawned a number of modern appendages around its Victorian core—the science block, the gym, and also the theater, where Jack would be appearing as Hamlet in two weeks' time. It all seemed very normal. Just like all the other schools in the border country against which Angus regularly played rugby. There was one difference: Soonhope High housed the most advanced technology known to man—the working Taurus. A time machine. As a result, the site had tighter security than a nuclear missile base. But it was completely unobtrusive. And that was the idea. Nobody, apart from a select few teachers and staff—plus some members of the community—knew of the astonishing secret housed within.

Jack was pretty sure that no one had arrived at school in quite such style before. Pity there was nobody there to see it.

The helicopter touched down, and Jack, Angus, the Rector, and Inchquin climbed out.

In the distance, two familiar figures stood waiting to welcome them—their old friends, Tony Smith and Gordon MacFarlane. They waited at one of the school's side entrances. Tony took up almost the entire doorway. Gordon stood beside him—he was shorter but still built like a tank. Officially, they were the school janitors. But Jack and Angus had learned their true identity six months before. Along with Belstaff and Johnstone, they were part of VIGIL's elite security squad.

"Gentlemen, please escort these two through entrance B to the Situation Room. We will join you shortly."

"An escort—good," Angus replied. "You two should have blue flashing lights on your heads."

"That's funny. Look"—Gordon clutched his stomach with both hands—"I'm in stitches."

The Rector scowled. "Gentlemen, I would advise less levity. We have an extremely serious situation here. Do I make myself clear?"

Gordon looked at his toes sheepishly. "Yes, sir. Sorry, sir."

Jack and Angus followed Tony and Gordon into the school.

"Here we are," Tony announced.

They had reached a closet halfway along one of the main corridors, and Tony proceeded to take a large set of keys from his belt, jangling them loudly as he searched for the right one.

"Isn't that a bit low-tech for VIGIL?"

"Now, son," Tony replied in a hushed voice, "you know better than to mention that name in an open area—even if no one else is here. Anyway, it's all part of our image; you're not supposed to see all the high-tech stuff."

Tony located the key, inserted it into the lock, and opened the door. The cupboard smelled of, well, school—that stale, dusty smell of textbooks, old pieces of computer equipment, and stationery. Tony reached inside his pocket and pulled out a thin piece of plastic that looked like a pocket calculator. He gently pressed a button on the device, and the closet door closed automatically behind them.

"That looks more like it," Angus said knowingly.

"I think this procedure will be familiar to you all. Step to the back, please." Tony pressed the device in his hand a second time, and without warning an aperture formed in the floor. Soon the entrance had opened completely, and a steep spiral staircase appeared, leading downward. It was lit by a ghostly blue glow, just bright enough for the boys to make out the position of the steps.

"OK, all clear. Down you go."

One by one, they stepped onto the spiral staircase. The steps began to descend automatically. As they dropped beneath floor level, the aperture above them closed silently, and after a couple of minutes they came to a gentle halt. Tony pressed the device again and the door ahead of them opened onto a short, metal-clad corridor illuminated by the same dim blue light. At the end of the corridor was a circular door resembling the entrance to a bank vault. It had five letters etched on it: **V I G I L.**

The door opened without a sound, revealing a tubular passageway that curved off symmetrically both to the left and to the right. Jack noticed that there were no markings on the passage walls—no rivets, no seams—it was perfectly, uncannily smooth.

"To your left, please," Tony said. They followed obediently and as they walked, the passageway bent away from the entrance, which resealed itself silently behind them. They had only taken twenty or thirty paces when Jack noticed a strange marking on the wall at about head height. It looked like the outline of a figure—a stylized hominid figure of some sort. There was something otherworldly about the marking. Jack stopped and turned to Tony.

"What does that symbol mean, Mr. Smith?"

Tony stopped suddenly and approached the figure on the wall. He turned to Gordon. "Have you seen this, MacFarlane?" he said apprehensively.

Gordon moved closer and inspected the strange marking, running his fingers tentatively over it. "Mmmm—the latest experiments must be more advanced than we thought."

Tony turned back to Jack and Angus. "VIGIL has been using their wormhole technology to experiment on new applications."

The boys' eyes widened.

"Yes, the figure on the door is indeed a symbol. . . ."

"The alien symbol," Gordon added reverentially.

"Signifying a portal to a whole new universe."

Angus's eyes widened. "You mean . . . space travel?"

Tony put them out of their misery. "No, you idiot, that's the men's toilet, and the ladies' is opposite—look. Do you need to go?"

Gordon laughed raucously, and the boys replied self-consciously, "We're fine, thanks."

The party moved on, Tony and Gordon much buoyed by their joke at the boys' expense.

Finally Tony announced, "OK, here we are."

The passageway had continued to curve around, and they had reached another doorway. Jack reckoned that if they continued on they would eventually rejoin where they had originally entered the underground complex. Essentially, they were in a giant subterranean donut, from which all the various VIGIL control rooms and annexes could be accessed.

Jack read the lettering on the door: SITUATION ROOM.

He felt his heartbeat tick up a notch. This was it.

Tony pressed the device in his hand, and the door slid open.

On each wall of the large underground room there were screens—some showed maps, some complex-looking historical timelines, and others just row upon row of computer programming language that Jack could not even begin to understand. Most of the VIGIL team was already seated around a large central board table, like a war council, but others manned computer terminals or other scientific equipment at pods in separate areas of the room.

Jack spotted a number of familiar faces: Miss Beattie, their English teacher, was in an animated conversation with, of all people, Gino

Turinelli, from the café on High Street. Jim de Raillar, who ran the mountain-bike shop two doors down from Gino's, was also there, and finally, Jack's mother, Carole, sat at one of the computer terminals. In fact, as Jack looked around he recognized everyone, and they all either worked at the school or in the local village of Soonhope. Since their inauguration into VIGIL, Jack had learned that VIGIL's network was quite pervasive and extended into the local community, but even then he had only met a few of the members. It made sense that there were many more. Clearly, you would need a lot of different skills to create and maintain a working time machine—and even more if you ever happened to use it. Each member of VIGIL had his or her everyday persona—whether it was a teacher, shopkeeper, janitor, or some such, and then the other—secret—role in the VIGIL organization: scientist, analyst, technician, or security guard. For example, Jack learned that Miss Beattie was not just an expert on Shakespeare, but had degrees from Cambridge and MIT. Gino—actually *Professor* Turinelli—was a computer expert, and Jim de Raillar and Carole, Jack's mom, were analysts.

Just then, the Rector and Inchquin came into the room through a separate entrance. Soon a tense discussion was underway, facilitated by Inchquin, who sat gravely at the head of the table.

"Jim, can you give us an update on the analysis of Tom Christie's message to us from a couple of hours ago, please?"

"Certainly. To recap, the message confirms that Christie and Dr. Pendelshape have fallen out. It also explains that following their failure to stop the First World War, they started to work on a new timeline simulation some months ago."

"What period does the simulation focus on?"

"Late Elizabethan."

"Interesting . . ." Theo Joplin, the historical analyst, interjected, and the Rector flashed him an angry glance for interrupting.

Jim de Raillar ignored the interchange and continued. "Anyway, it appears that the Revisionist team has refined the computer simulation software so that they can make much more precise re-creations of how interventions can be made in history, and their consequences. Christie's message referred to this as 'surgical' historical modeling. It seems that the Revisionist team was very excited about these advances, but then Christie got nervous when Pendelshape started to talk in terms of progressing the simulation to the implementation phase—an actual intervention in history. Pendelshape wanted to target the late sixteenth century using their replica Taurus. Of course, it was clear from the message that Christie does not want the Revisionists to do this. . . ." De Raillar paused and looked at Inchquin and then at Carole and Jack uneasily. There was an edgy silence in the room.

"Go on."

"Well, it appears that Pendelshape and the rest of the Revisionists have no such concerns, and it looks like they have decided to go forward anyway, so Christie felt that the Revisionists were moving against him and left them some weeks ago. Concerned that they would quickly refine the simulation and we might think him responsible, he took the unprecedented step of sending us a warning message today—and then contacting Jack. It is a big step for him. Christie knows he is risking his life by betraying his own team in such a way. He is now isolated from both VIGIL and the Revisionists."

Inchquin arched his fingers in front of him, deep in thought. "So, Pendelshape has usurped Tom Christie as the leader of the Revisionists. He has a plan to make an intervention in history during the sixteenth century. Two things to check. First, Carole, what is the latest forecast on time signal availability?"

Carole looked up from her terminal. "We have had no time signal availability for a number of weeks now, but as you are aware, we are forecasting the availability of time travel signals of carrier strength over the next forty-eight hours. Although, as you know, forecasts are not accurate—in terms of timing, duration, or strength."

"Time-signal forecasting—it's worse than the weather forecast . . ." Joplin moaned.

"Theo, you're not helping," the Rector said. "This is why Christie has chosen to contact us now. The Revisionists will also know that we are entering a period of potential time signal availability, so Christie must think they will use this opportunity to carry out their plan." He paused. "Do we have any details on the actual intervention in history that they are planning?"

"No. Apparently when Christie left, there were a number of open scenarios still being analyzed—but they were not complete. He had no final detailed plans."

"So, Theo, now is the time to say something sensible. You're the historian; any particular views on why they would choose that period of history to make an intervention—between 1580 and 1600?"

Theo Joplin looked up from a laptop that he had open in front of him. He was only twenty-seven but looked like a relic of sixties hippiedom with his long hair, goatee, and flowery shirt. But appearances were deceptive, and encased within his mop of messy black hair was an encyclopedic knowledge of history.

Joplin curled his lip. "A good choice if you want to make some structural changes to the future course of history—many, many options, lots going on, overall, a very cool period." He turned back to his laptop, assuming that this would be a more than sufficient contribution to the conversation.

The Rector tried to contain his frustration. "Would you mind being a little more *specific*?"

Joplin shrugged nonchalantly. "English Renaissance, Shakespeare, Marlowe, Spanish Armada—or Armadas, I should say—Mary, Queen of Scots, the Babington Plot, the Player's Plot, Drake, Raleigh, Howard, Grenville, treasure fleets, first English colony in America, religious conflict, Ireland . . . I could go on . . . and no doubt you want me to . . ."

"We don't have time for all this," Inchquin said irritably. "Jim, are we sure that Christie's message did not say anything more specific about what Pendelshape and the other Revisionists might be trying to do?"

"He said that Pendelshape had a well-developed theory that if the Spanish dominance of the period could have been extended somehow, then it could have been harnessed to usher in a period of peace. Perhaps for centuries. A strong Spain would have defeated the Netherlands and then colonized all of the Americas . . . and also

31

they would have been better able to enforce a single religion—Catholicism. This would have reduced religious conflict."

"Interesting theory," Joplin piped up, suddenly interested. "It's true that the period was a bit of a turning point for Spain. She was the most powerful country in the world, but from that point her power declined gradually."

"Since when, specifically?"

"The defeat of the Armada, really, in 1588. The fact that Queen Elizabeth reigned for so long as a Protestant queen, and the fact that the Armada failed meant that the balance of power—certainly naval power—slowly transferred to Britain. So Britain by the nineteenth century was the most powerful nation on earth."

"So you're saying that without Elizabeth, then the world would have been a different place."

"Very different. The common language of the West would be Spanish, not English—just as it is in much of South America today. The influence of Protestantism would have been substantially weaker, and we would have many different habits and customs. We might even have a regular bullfight in Soonhope." Joplin chortled.

"Theo, this is not funny," Inchquin growled. "Jim, do you think that is what Pendelshape is trying to do?"

"Something like that—it lines up with what Christie told us. But the details were not fully developed when Christie left. The main thing he wanted to make clear was that he just did not want to be associated with any of it—and more than that, he wanted us to know that he was not associated with it. So that we would not take . . . retribution . . . on him." Jim paused and then added bluntly, "Or his family."

"I understand," Inchquin said, moving on swiftly. "Well, we really need more data than this—it is all too sketchy at the moment. Tony, can you radio the team up on the hill? Perhaps they have managed to track him down . . ."

Suddenly Carole called out from behind her terminal. "Counselor, there is some sort of reading. We have an emerging time signal. It's faint but it looks like there is a deep time disturbance . . . possibly time travel initiation. "

"Can you pinpoint it?"

"Difficult to identify the travel precisely—but the impacted year is 1587. Looks to be early that year."

"Location?"

"England—definitely. Southeast. Must be London."

"Well, that decides it then. It looks like Christie was right and the Revisionists are making their move. We must not waste any more time. We need to mobilize immediately." Inchquin rose to his feet and placed both palms on the table, his voice grave.

"I feared it would only be a matter of time before this would happen again. Everyone, security protocol is Triple Alpha. VIGIL is now on high alert. You all know what to do."

Sixteenth-Century Sortie

Jack stood before the Taurus feeling several emotions, not all of them good. Last time he had been in the Taurus control room, he had thought he was going to die. The Taurus loomed ominously behind a solid wall of thick green glass that extended from the floor all the way up to the ceiling. The great machine had been expanded and rebuilt since he had seen it last. From their previous mission, VIGIL had learned that the Revisionists' Taurus was significantly larger than VIGIL's and had the capability to transport sizeable items of machinery, as well as people. It was prudent for VIGIL's Taurus to have a similar capability—just in case. This was despite the fact that VIGIL would only ever use their machine for emergencies such as this, and was reluctant to transfer equipment that was potentially out of period because of the consequences this could have in changing history. As they had learned, the Revisionists were not so fussy.

The great machine sat brooding among an arrangement of complex engineering equipment, pipes, cables, and access gantries. The shell of the Taurus itself was a raised metal platform bounded by a semiclosed arrangement of eight hefty black moveable metal struts. They rose from the ground and bulged out to surround the platform and then rejoined each other at the top. The simplicity of this inner structure belied the wonder and complexity of its function.

The VIGIL team quickly developed a plan based on piecing together the little information that they had gleaned from Christie's message to VIGIL. A party of four would be transported to February 1587 to attempt to locate and intercept Pendelshape before he carried out the Revisionists' plan. This would not be easy since the details of his intent and his location were still sketchy. The search party on the hill had reported back, and so far there had been no sign of Tom Christie—and it was unlikely he would contact VIGIL again; there was too high a risk that he might reveal his own whereabouts, and regardless, it sounded like he only knew the outline of the Revisionists' plan. Nevertheless, Inchquin had instructed the search party to continue through the night.

The time travel team—Tony, Gordon, Jim de Raillar, and Theo Joplin—had been dispatched to the preparation annex for equipment allocation and further briefing. It was not clear to Jack what would be done with Pendelshape in the event that he was found by the VIGIL squad that was about to be sent back, but Jack suspected that it would not be pleasant.

Inchquin had issued orders to power up the Taurus, and remaining VIGIL team members had already arrived to support the emergency mission. Everyone seemed to be well-drilled—emergencies like this were something that they now practiced for repeatedly, ever since the events that had occurred six months ago. The control room itself had morphed into a command center—the nearest thing Jack could think to compare it to was NASA mission control. Jack and Angus sat in an observation area within the control room. Angus followed the proceedings with great excitement and would occasionally nudge Jack and point something out as the transfer time drew close.

As they watched, a door at the far end of the control center opened when the VIGIL response squad arrived from the preparation annex, ready for boarding the Taurus.

"Best I could do, I'm afraid," Joplin announced.

The response squad needed to be fully prepared for the Elizabethan period. They had to ensure that they would not inadvertently trigger something—however small—that might have further effects on the future. If they did, this might mean that VIGIL would need to return to repair the damage—in itself a risky scenario. They needed to try and blend in. At the basic level this meant wearing the right clothes. VIGIL had built up an extensive costume archive for this purpose—it had the benefit of doubling as the school's wardrobe for the English and drama departments.

The response squad stepped forward, somewhat sheepishly, to display the fruits of their efforts. Tony and de Raillar looked reasonable. They wore snug black doublets with jerkins on top and short cloaks. Beneath their cloaks each wore a thin backpack that contained a range of equipment for their mission—including basic provisions. On their legs they wore breeches, which were pinned in at the knee. Each wore a dagger on a belt. Joplin, however, was a different matter. He looked like one of the Three Musketeers. He wore a loose-fitting doublet with baggy trousers that were tucked in at boot level and a long cloak that was elaborately embroidered and worn jauntily off one shoulder. On his head he wore a ridiculous wide-brimmed hat adorned with a long plume of feathers, and on his feet he wore riding boots with wide turnovers trimmed with lace. Finally, from a broad leather belt hung a full length sword.

"It's about forty years too late for the period, but it's all we could find in the wardrobe," he announced.

But the best was still to come.

A moment later Gordon appeared and Jack and Angus burst out laughing. Gordon also wore a tight doublet on his upper body, but it was far too small for his powerful frame. The garment had elaborate inlays and patterns, and at the collar Gordon wore an intricate lace ruff which seemed to push his chin upward at an alarming angle. On his legs, he wore enormous baggy breeches which ballooned out from his waist and were gathered in at midthigh level. These were highly decorated in a night-scape of yellow half-moons and stars. Beneath the flouncy breeches, Gordon was actually wearing tights. *Bright yellow tights.* These encased a pair of powerful legs that were more used to pumping iron than mincing around an Elizabethan royal court. To finish it off, Gordon wore white shoes, open on each side . . . and—this was the final straw for Angus and Jack—flowers were pinned to the front. A lot of flowers.

Inchquin put his head in his hands. Gordon shrugged. "We ran out—had to move on to the aristocrats' section. . . . At least I'm in period."

The Rector sighed. "You'll just have to see what you can lay your hands on when you get there."

Everything was finally in place, and the Rector completed the final briefing. "Any questions before we initiate final countdown sequence?"

Angus nudged Jack. He had a warped smile on his face, the kind that Jack knew typically meant only one thing—trouble.

Jack mouthed, "What?"

But before he could stop him, Angus was marching over to the Rector and Inchquin. "What about us?" he demanded.

Jack cringed. Without hesitation, Inchquin immediately replied, "Out of the question."

But Angus was not about to be patronized. "So why are we in VIGIL at all, then? You have always said that one of the main points of VIGIL is to prepare the next generation, you know, to protect history and protect the human race, and how can we do that if we are stuck here—just watching?"

Suddenly, support piped up for Angus from an unexpected source—Miss Beattie. "You know, the lad has a point. He's young, he's extremely fit, and has already proved himself on one mission."

"Yes, sir," Angus said. "I thought that's what I was here for, you know, to help."

Inchquin looked at the Rector and Miss Beattie nervously. "I'm not sure we can authorize . . . we are not really in a position . . ."

Angus interrupted him. "But you said yourself—VIGIL can decide whatever it wants."

Inchquin looked to his fellow VIGIL colleagues, waiting to see if any would voice an opinion. There was silence.

Angus's outburst had gotten Jack thinking—but not quite along the same lines as his friend. He spoke up. "Sir, I don't entirely agree with Angus—I mean time traveling again would be pretty scary. But there is one thing. Angus and I know Pendelshape well. And we also know that Pendelshape was desperate to get us to join him and Dad. I know Dad has had a falling-out with Pendelshape. But maybe if we were to go back as part of the team, maybe there will be a chance we could link up with Pendelshape and, well, pretend we wanted to come over to his side—you know, because of Dad or something. With us under his control, Pendelshape would think he could get Dad to rejoin them. What I am trying to say is . . ."

Inchquin finished Jack's sentence. "Pendelshape might trust you . . . and we could use that to stop Pendelshape and infiltrate the Revisionists."

"And finish them off for good," the Rector added. He nodded thoughtfully. "It certainly gives us another option."

Angus punched the air. "Yes!"

Inchquin smiled. "I guess you can take de Raillar and Joplin's places and they can form the next wave—your backup, if it's needed."

Jack's mom had been following the discussion with increasing dismay. "I can't possibly agree to this," she blurted out.

But the words tumbled from Jack's mouth before he had time to stop them: "Mom, sorry, I've been thinking about it. The Christie family is partly responsible for all of this. If it's anyone's duty to help sort this out, it's ours or at least, mine."

It was decided.

Thirty minutes later Jack, Angus, Tony, and Gordon stood on the Taurus platform. Miss Beattie's costumes for the production of *Hamlet* were raided in order to clothe Jack and Angus in period. Beneath their woollen cloaks they each carried one of the thin VIGIL backpacks. Under their doublets they wore tight-fitting vests and in these were secreted the all-important time phones. The countdown was already under way, and the assembled VIGIL team looked on from their positions behind the blast screen. The Rector was completing a short lecture, reminding them of the workings of the Taurus. Not that Jack needed reminding.

"Remember, the Taurus itself stays here—it focuses the energy and creates the temporary wormhole. But to move through time and space, you need to have physical contact with a time phone. You need one to go . . . and to get back. While back in time, the time phone is controlled and tracked by the Taurus. Of course, it will only work when the Taurus is at the right energy state, and also when there is a strong enough time signal, like a cell phone, and the signals are intermittent. Remember that bar?" He prodded the little grayed-out display inside the time phone. "When it's yellow, you're good to go—you can communicate, we know where you are, and the Taurus can send you back and forth through time. When there's no signal, you're stuck—although the phone's energy source will continue to tell you where and when you are." Finally, the Rector said ominously, "Lose your time phones and there is no way back."

Jack was sweating. He could hear the high-pitched whine from the powerful generators even though they were well-insulated within the underground complex. He glanced at Angus, who stood next to him on the platform and was grinning insanely, still not believing his luck. He didn't seem to be remotely concerned that he was about to be flushed down a wormhole to 400 years in the past and a world that they would find totally alien. In front of them, Jack could see the small heads-up display. Taurus was counting down:

10 . . . 9 . . . 8 . . .

The last time this had happened, Jack had been so frightened, he had not noticed the physical changes in the Taurus chamber around him as they approached the event horizon—the point of no return. Around his feet he could see shimmering eddies of light. He supposed they were some sort of electrical disturbance, a bit like the ion-charged curtains of blue, red, and green of the northern lights. The shimmering became stronger, and it was as if he were standing in the rippling waters of an illuminated whirlpool. The atmosphere within the Taurus structure was also changing, and the control room beyond appeared darker and fuzzier—as if you were looking at a badly tuned TV screen.

Suddenly, through the blast screen, he saw the Rector draw his hand dramatically across his throat, as if to say stop. He was shouting and waving frantically, and immediately there was a flurry of activity in the control room. The Rector's distorted words came through the audio feed.

"Abort! Abort!"

There was something wrong. But the countdown continued relentlessly.

7 . . . 6 . . . 5 . . . 4 . . .

Jack felt panic surge through his body, and he glanced over at Tony and Gordon for guidance. But there was nothing they could do. They could hear the Rector's voice, desperately shouting, "Abort system! Time-fix malfunction . . . abort this mission—NOW!"

3 . . . 2 . . . 1 . . .

Jack looked down. Suddenly the flashing electrical whirlpool beneath them vanished, and they stared down into a black abyss.

The last thing he heard was his mom scream, "Jack!"

Keep Your Head

Jack opened his eyes. He was prostrate and stared into a bleak, gray sky. Suddenly, three large golden lions floated gently across his field of vision. Jack blinked. It had happened. He was dead and in heaven, where mystical golden lions were flying across the sky. . . .

"Get up!"

Angus's ruddy face loomed over him as he shook Jack by the shoulders.

Jack blinked again. Then he understood. He was staring at a giant flag that fluttered in a strong, wintry breeze just above their heads. The flag was split into quadrants—the upper left and lower right quadrants had a dark blue background, and each displayed three identical symbols that looked a bit like flowers. The two other quadrants each had a crimson background, and on these were painted the three golden lions. Jack recognized the design of the flag from Miss Beattie's book. They were English lions and French fleur-de-lis. The English royal standard.

"I have no idea where we are, but there are loads of people down there . . ."

Jack pulled himself to his feet and rubbed his head. He felt like he'd been hit by a truck.

"What's going on?"

But Jack was silenced by the view before him. It took his breath away. They were perched on top of a vertiginous crenulated tower, which rose high above one side of a massive medieval castle. They could see for miles in every direction—a flat, sparse landscape of muddy fields, marshes, and scattered woodland. There was no foliage on the trees, and it was bitterly cold. The stonework beneath their feet was wet from a recent downpour. Over a hundred feet below them a slow-moving river meandered gently through the countryside. Nearby, there was a fine stone church with flying buttresses and a distinctive octagonal tower. Jack could also see a large crowd of people stretching from the entrance to the castle all the way back along a path toward a small village. The crowd was being chaperoned by men on horseback, and Jack could see that some people in the crowd were holding placards, as if they were at a demonstration. It was difficult to make out what was on the placards, but there was one large one near the front that seemed to have a picture on it. It was bizarre, but Jack could have sworn it depicted a mermaid.

"Where are we? What happened?" Jack said woozily.

"Don't know. I think we passed out. My head's thumping."

"Something went wrong."

"You can say that again. Tony and Gordon have disappeared, unless they landed somewhere nearby . . ."

"Are they dead?"

"No idea."

"So we're on our own?"

"Looks like it. Some malfunction."

Jack's heart sank when the reality of their situation dawned on him. He gritted his teeth and swallowed.

"Well, we'd better get a grip. We're full-fledged members of VIGIL now. Have you looked at your time phone?"

Angus slipped his hand beneath his cloak and inside the doublet provided by VIGIL into the breast pocket of his undervest. He unzipped a padded pouch and removed the precious time phone. He cupped it in his hands and flicked it open. A faint blue light illuminated the device from the inside. They inspected the readout.

```
Date:      Wednesday, February 8, 1587
Time:      9:45 a.m.
Location:  Fotheringhay, England
```

"Well, the Taurus has dumped us back in 1587, all right. . . ."

Angus looked over the parapet. "But this definitely isn't London. No red buses, for a start."

"Ha. Maybe that's why they tried to abort the mission? The Taurus must have put us here by mistake. . . . Maybe it even split us up and put Tony and Gordon in the right place."

Angus groaned. "Well, what do we do now?"

"Is there a signal?"

They peered at the time phone again. The telltale bar that burned bright yellow when there was a time signal was grayed out—dead. The boys knew what that meant. They were stuck, and they could not communicate with VIGIL. It was impossible to tell how long it would stay that way.

"Well, that's great. We're toast. Already." Angus said bitterly. "So much for VIGIL."

"Let's have a look at the readout again."

Jack studied the readout and pondered its meaning. "Fotheringhay."

Angus cocked his head. "Where is Fotheringhay, anyway?"

"I'm not sure. I think it's in Cambridgeshire or something. I'm sure this place is famous . . . but I can't remember why."

"Well, we can't hang around here much longer. I'm freezing my butt off."

Angus was right. The adrenaline had finally worn off and they were beginning to feel the chill from the cold morning. If it rained again, it might even turn into snow. They needed shelter.

"Down there, I suppose?" Angus nodded toward a small arched oak door built into the tower.

"Probably. I don't know what choice we have. Judging from that crowd, there seems to be some sort of event going on in the castle. Maybe it's a wedding or something. We should be able to sneak out through the crowd."

"Then what?"

Jack shrugged. "I don't know. We probably need to try and hide somewhere until we get a time signal and can communicate with VIGIL. But you're right, we can't stay up here, or we'll freeze to death."

The squat wooden door opened onto a dank spiral staircase, and the boys started to make their way down. As they descended, occasionally a slit window would give them a view of the large courtyard at the center of the castle. It was busy. There were tethered horses being tended by servants, breastplated soldiers, and finely attired gentlemen who talked conspiratorially in small groups. Toward one end, a large bonfire was being built, and in a corner there was a gathering of musicians who played a depressing dirge.

"Doesn't sound much like wedding music."

"No—and there are lots of guards or soldiers around, so something's going on."

"And that flag," Jack added. "I'm pretty sure that's the royal flag, so maybe it's a special occasion?"

"A royal visit? Now that would be something to tell Joplin—his goatee would fall off," Angus said.

They finally reached the bottom of the tower, which opened through a large oak door onto a stone-flagged corridor. They followed the corridor, and after a while they could hear hushed voices. Ahead was a thick curtain. They looked at each other. There was only one way for them to go—they slipped behind the curtain.

They found themselves to the rear of a dense crowd in a great hall. People seemed to be jostling for position. Something—or someone—was commanding a lot of interest, and the arrival of Jack and Angus went unnoticed. Soon, more people joined the crowd, and they felt themselves being pushed farther forward with the throng. There was wood smoke in the air from log fires burning in the hall. It mingled with the smell of woollen cloaks still wet from the early morning rain. With his height, Angus might be able to see what was going on, but Jack could see nothing—just the press of bodies in front of him. He was propelled forward by pushing from behind and then, all of a sudden, he was at the front.

Below a great vaulted roof, a wooden platform had been constructed which was fringed with black material. It looked about twenty feet across and maybe a couple of feet high. It reminded Jack of the stage on which they would be performing *Hamlet* back at Soonhope, but it didn't seem likely that these people were there to watch a play.

Quite unexpectedly, from one side of the hall, three men appeared, walking slowly. They were dressed in fine clothes and they looked important. The man in front carried a slender white stick. A tall woman walked slowly behind them with her head down. Her auburn hair peeked out from behind a head scarf. She was clad from head to foot in black velvet and a golden cross hung around her neck. When she appeared, the entire hall went silent.

The woman mounted the steps of the dais and walked to a high backed chair which was also draped in black. In front of the chair was a cushion and in front of that a simple wooden block with a half-moon shape cut into its upper section. Two large, powerfully built men stood on either side of her. They reminded Jack of Tony and Gordon, but they were dressed entirely in black and wore masks. Angus peered at Jack with a quizzical look on his face; he had no idea what was going on. But Jack only needed one glance at what one of the masked men was holding to confirm what he already knew. Both his hands rested on the wooden handle of a large double-headed ax.

To their right a clerk unrolled a parchment and started to read. The language was complicated but Jack caught snippets as the charge was read out: "Stubborn disobedience . . . incitement to insurrection . . . person of Her Sacred Majesty."

The pieces of the jigsaw came together in Jack's head—the place: Fotheringhay Castle; the date: February 8th, 1587; the crime: high treason; the punishment: death by beheading. Jack now even understood the significance of the placards outside the castle. The crowd outside was making its feelings clear about the prisoner before them in the great hall. Jack and Angus were about to witness the execution of Mary, Queen of Scots—cousin of Queen Elizabeth I and enemy of the English state.

The executioner and the assistant knelt before the queen to ask forgiveness. From where he stood, Jack could hear her reply word for

The execution of Mary, Queen of Scots, February 8, 1587

word: "I forgive you with all my heart, for now, I hope, you shall make an end of all my troubles." Her ladies-in-waiting stepped forward to help her remove her gown. Beneath it she wore a petticoat of red satin—crimson, the martyrs' color. Next she took the gold cross from her neck and handed it to the executioner, who slipped it into his shoe, claiming the executioner's right to the personal property of the condemned.

She knelt on the cushion and put her head on the block. Jack wanted to scream and turn and run. But the scene before them had a peculiar, hypnotic momentum, and he was rooted to the spot— compelled to see the horror through to its conclusion. The white nape of the queen's neck stretched over the coarse wooden block for all to see. It looked strangely fragile and slender. She stretched out her hands on either side of her in the pose of Jesus, crucified on the cross. The executioner wielded the massive ax and it glinted momentarily in the firelight and then wheeled downward with terrifying speed. The noise that the ax made on impact was one that Jack would never forget.

But the blow had failed to sever the head from the body completely, and the executioner repeated the procedure. His job completed, he lifted the head from the floor and held it high, crying, "God save the Queen!" There was a ripple of noise through the crowd. The executioner was only holding Mary's auburn wig, and the head, shaved to a gray stubble, had dropped to the platform and rolled forward before coming to rest just a few feet away from where Jack and Angus stood. The pale eyes in the head were still open, and they stared straight at them.

Escape

The bonfire in the courtyard was blazing, and the crowd watched as Mary's garments were dispatched onto it. Everything stained with her blood was to be burned to prevent the items from being used as the holy relics of a martyr. Angus turned to Jack and spoke for the first time since witnessing the horror of the execution. His voice trembled.

"You're going to have to explain to me what just happened . . ."

"But not now; we need to get out of here first."

"What about one of those?"

Angus nodded at one of the horses lined up along one side of the courtyard. A number of them were saddled, ready for the gentry and noblemen to return home.

"I forgot you could ride."

"Of course I can ride—I live on a farm."

"But I can't."

"It's easy—you just sit back. The horse does the rest."

"That's what I thought you might say. Anyway, those horses don't belong to us."

Angus shrugged and turned back to the fire. Its warmth was little comfort.

"We need to do something. This crowd's starting to thin down— soon we'll be noticed. I've already gotten some funny looks."

They looked around furtively. Across the other side of the courtyard, next to a large arched doorway, they spied a group of noblemen together with some servants. Jack jumped out of his skin when one of the servants appeared to point them out to an older, official-looking man. A moment later three guards appeared from the doorway brandishing halberds. They advanced toward them.

"I don't like the look of this."

"Neither do I. . . . Let's not hang around."

Without hesitation Angus sprinted toward one of the tethered horses. He untied it and, with impressive athleticism, jumped up onto its back.

There was a cry from the approaching soldiers.

"Stop them! Spies!"

Angus wheeled the horse around, "Come on! Get up, or we're done!"

Jack had no idea what to do, having never been on a horse in his life. "But . . ."

"Give me your hand."

Angus reached down with a swarthy arm and hauled Jack up toward him. To his great surprise, a moment later Jack found himself plonked high up on the rear of the horse behind Angus.

Angus wheeled the horse around and kicked his heels in. The poor beast reared up and for a moment Jack thought he was going to slide off—but then they rebalanced and the horse shot off at a gallop toward the castle gate. The remaining people in the courtyard leaped aside as they careered forward. Jack shut his eyes and clung on. There was more shouting from behind them. Jack braced himself—surely he was about to get an arrow between his shoulder blades. But they raced through the open gate and charged along the lane that led up toward the village. Jack twisted around to see whether they were being followed. For a moment he saw nothing, but then a posse of four riders raced through the gate in hot pursuit.

He yelled forward to Angus, "They're following us!"

"Hang on!"

Angus spurred the horse again, and it pounded onward. Jack felt that at any moment he was going to fall off.

The village of Fotheringhay was small, but its population had been swelled by the dramatic events of the morning, and its main street was swarming with people, animals, and carts of all sorts. Angus slowed down, but not by much, and miraculously they managed to slalom their way through the throng. As they reached the far side of the village, Jack snatched a second look behind. The pursuing horsemen were still there—and they were getting closer.

He thumped Angus on the back. "They're gaining!"

The river came back into view on the left of the path. It was slow-moving, but brown and swollen from the winter rain.

"Hold on!" Angus shouted. In a second they plunged into the icy water. The cold took Jack's breath away. But the water only came up to their thighs, and soon the horse found its footing on the bottom of the river. Angus made noises of encouragement—spurring the beast on. As they approached the opposite bank the current eased and the water became shallower. The horse sensed safety and pressed on energetically. They had made it.

Angus spun the horse around. Opposite, their pursuers had arrived at the embankment. Not to be outdone, two of the pursuing horsemen immediately attempted the same crossing. But the first horse slipped and its rider became unseated and fell into the mud, sliding headlong into the torrent. The second horse somehow became entangled in the first, and its rider was also thrown free. Soon both riders and horses were in the river and being swept along in the current. The remaining two horsemen were not about to risk the same fate, and they peered across the water in frustration as their prey, Jack and Angus, turned and galloped away to the woodland beyond.

The Fanshawe Players

The path became more gnarled and muddy the farther they traveled. It had been badly mauled by the wheels of carts and the hooves of horses, although Jack and Angus hadn't seen anyone for at least two hours. A weak winter sun filtered through the oak branches above, but it brought no warmth, and Jack's legs remained horribly cold from the dousing in the river. He was also aching from sitting awkwardly behind Angus on the horse, which had kept going, despite all the abuse thrown at it.

"Who knows what they would have done if they caught up to us?"

"Probably a quick beheading."

"What do you think they wanted, anyway?"

Jack shrugged. "I don't know. But they figured out that we were strangers . . ."

"The guy said *spy*. Why did he think that?"

"This is England, 1587, Angus. The Queen has just ordered the execution of Mary, Queen of Scots, her own cousin. Mary was accused of a plot to overthrow Elizabeth, and I think there are plots going on all the time. Probably everyone is paranoid and jumpy . . . and with good reason. I read that the execution is the last excuse the king of Spain needs to launch the Armada—you know, to try and get rid of Elizabeth and Protestant England for good."

"I've got to tell you, I'm not really bothered about all that. I want to get warm, get some food, and wait for a time signal so we can make contact with VIGIL." Angus dismounted and patted the horse's gray flank. "Good boy."

"You can get off now, Jack. I think this guy's gone as far as he can." Angus patted the horse again. "What should we do with him?"

"Let him go—he'll probably find his way back, right?" Angus said.

"Or someone will pick him up. He's valuable."

Angus slapped the rear of the horse, and it trotted off back down the path. Jack looked around. The woodland was particularly thick here. There were a number of old oaks with impressively broad trunks. Even though it was winter and there was little foliage, they could not see through the woods more than about fifty yards in any one direction. It was eerily quiet.

"Hey, do your ears feel funny, Jack?" Angus put a finger in one ear and rubbed vigorously.

"Sort of—but I think I know what it is. That won't help. It's nothing. I mean literally nothing. There's no noise. No ambient noise. Usually in towns and cities and even in the countryside where we live back home there is always some noise—like from cars, planes, machinery, and stuff. Usually you just don't notice it—but it's always there, in the background. Here, there's none of that. It's perfectly silent. So it seems weird to us. It almost sounds like there *is* noise."

"Well whatsit noise or not, we need to push on for a couple of miles and then maybe turn off the road and go deeper into these woods. Find a spot to hide and wait—maybe try and get a fire going and dry out—until we get a signal, or until we run out of food packets. I'm hungry, but we'll need to ration them out."

They continued up the path, trying to avoid the worst of the puddles and the mud, but progress was slow and soon their boots squelched in the muddy water. After an hour, Jack was ready to give up when they rounded a bend that curved down to a small clearing in the woods. There was a crossroads where another muddy path intersected with theirs. A wooden cart, like a gypsy caravan, stood by the path. It was the first sign of life they had seen since Fotheringhay. They approached cautiously. As they drew near to the back of the cart they could hear a sound: snoring.

Suddenly, a man's face appeared from behind the canvas cover at the rear of the cart. It was a round face with red cheeks, and it was cocked to one side. Rather oddly, the man was wearing a large, floppy jester's hat decorated with bright red and yellow stripes. It even had bells on it.

"Fanshawe! Monk! Get up!" he shouted in a squeaky voice. "We have visitors."

There was a commotion inside the cart, and it creaked on its wheels. A donkey chomped disinterestedly on the remains of the thin grass at its feet nearby. Then the faces of two other men popped out from behind the canvas cover. One was bald and had a fringe of straight black hair all the way around his head. The other was more distinguished looking and had a finely trimmed mustache and a pointed beard. He spoke in a rich voice and carefully enunciated each syllable.

"What have we here?"

Soon the strange trio of gentlemen was outside the cart and inspecting Jack and Angus with interest. The one with the jester's hat was actually wearing a full jester's outfit with a diamond patterned overcoat and pixie boots, which also had bells attached to the toes. The bald one was dressed in the opposite way and wore a simple brown cassock tied with a rope around his waist. The one with the beard—who seemed to be in charge—was dressed like a country gentleman with a doublet and hose, but he did sport a rather dashing green cloak.

"An audience, perchance," he said.

Jack replied nervously, "Er, sorry, sir, we don't have any money . . ."

"We're on our way to . . ." But Angus didn't know where they could be on their way to and looked at Jack for inspiration.

Jack had a brain wave. "To Cambridge. We are . . . scholars. Returning scholars."

"Well, there is a bit of luck—we are going to Cambridge as well," the man announced. He slapped his friend with the cassock on the back; the other man just stood there grumpily. "Monk, what do you think of that? These fine young men also journey to the fine city of Cambridge. Isn't that indeed providential?"

At this exciting news the jester whipped out one yellow and one red handkerchief and proceeded to perform an astonishingly stupid jig of joy in front of them. Angus tried not to laugh.

"We must be introduced. I am Harry Fanshawe"—Fanshawe did an elaborate bow—"Leader of the Fanshawe Players. And this is Monk." Fanshawe elbowed the dour-looking man in the cassock, who, now that Jack thought about it, looked exactly like a monk. "Monk, try and be friendly." Monk grunted. "He's not a real monk, you know. . . . It is his persona. And this is Trinculo." The jester grinned at them and said, "At your service, sirs. Will it be comedy, tragedy, or poetry?"

"Actually, we could use something to eat," Angus said hopefully.

For some reason the previously dour Monk burst out in sarcastic laughter.

"That's the best idea I have heard for two days." He suddenly stopped laughing and looked up at Fanshawe accusingly. *"Is there* any chance of some food . . . or dare I even say it, money?"

Fanshawe shrugged his shoulders huffily. "Fine, then. I suppose I need to go and check the traps," he said, and marched off to the woods.

Despite the damp weather, Monk and Trinculo somehow managed to get a fire burning with kindling from the back of the wagon. Angus and Jack tried to help by gathering wood from the edge of the clearing. Although it was wet, the old stuff had been lying around for long enough that after the damp had smoked off, it caught fire, and soon Jack and Angus were trying to dry their feet while they waited for Fanshawe.

"He won't find anything," Monk moaned. "It's been two days now."

But then a triumphant Fanshawe appeared from a clearing, a brace of rabbits dangling from one hand.

"Providential!" he shouted.

Trinculo beamed. "Hallelujah!"

The rabbits were skinned at high speed—a spectacle that turned Jack's stomach, but seemed quite natural for Fanshawe, Monk, and Trinculo. Soon Monk was eagerly turning a makeshift spit suspended over the spluttering fire.

"So, gentlemen, you have not told us where you are from," Fanshawe said, eyeing them curiously.

Angus looked over at Jack. "Er . . . the North."

"That must explain your strange accent. . . . And which college in Cambridge will you be returning to?"

Again, Jack somehow came up with an answer, remembering a name from Miss Beattie's book.

"Queen's College."

"A glorious establishment. Providential," Fanshawe said.

"And yourselves . . . where will you be performing?"

Fanshawe beamed with pride at the question. "We shall be performing with my friend, the young genius, Christopher Marlowe."

Monk rolled his eyes cynically. "But he's not really your friend, is he?"

Fanshawe's eyes flashed in anger. "A curse on you, Monk—he is my friend, and he will welcome us with an open heart."

"Well, let's hope he does, because if he doesn't, that's the last straw and I'm off—like all the others before me." Monk turned his attention back to the spit.

"O ye of little faith," Fanshawe retorted pompously. "Anyway, gentlemen, Marlowe"—Fanshawe drilled his eyes into the back of Monk's head—"*my good friend,* will be performing his new play, *Tamburlaine the Great,* at his old college in Cambridge, Corpus Christi. And, what is more, he has invited the famous Fanshawe Players to join him. It is an opportunity of a lifetime."

"Opportunity of a lunchtime, more like," Monk said sulkily under his breath.

Fanshawe ignored the remark, then added conspiratorially, "I hope that I might even sell him some of my work . . ."

"Your work?"

"Plays, sonnets, and songs—a lifetime of toil and achievement. If I do say so myself."

Monk rolled his eyes a second time, and Trinculo interjected before Monk said anything to further antagonize Fanshawe, "I think those must be done by now."

The rabbit was removed from the spit and handed around. Jack and Angus exchanged glances, weighing if the meat would be safe, but the others were already munching happily away. Even Fanshawe had been momentarily silenced. Jack was so hungry he was past caring, and he popped the meat into his mouth. It tasted rich, gamey, and delicious.

In under a minute, the meat was gone, but it had scarcely made an impact on their hunger. Angus proceeded to rummage inside his tunic and withdrew a small plastic bag. Jack shot him a look, but it was too late and the brightly colored bag had already been spotted by the others.

"And what is this?" Trinculo asked. "An interesting bag of tricks?"

Angus looked down at the bag and suddenly realized his mistake. "Oh, sorry, a delicacy from our home, er, you know, in the North. You eat them."

"Do they have a name?"

Angus glanced nervously at Jack. "They're called gummy worms."

"Worms made of gum?" Trinculo asked.

"Which you eat?" Monk said in awe.

"It's just a name—try one." Angus passed the bag around and in trepidation, Trinculo, Fanshawe, and finally Monk each removed one of the colored sweets. They held them in their dirty fingers and waited for Angus to show them what to do. Angus shrugged and popped one into this mouth.

"There—nothing to it."

They each copied Angus, and as they chewed, expressions of wonder and appreciation spread across their faces.

"Sweet."

"Chewy."

"A most providential delicacy."

"Glad you like them. Here—have the rest."

The gummy worms were soon gone, and Angus had made friends for life.

Fanshawe, probably buoyed by the unexpected sugar high, leaped to his feet to continue where he had left off.

"My friends, I feel it is time for a song to celebrate our new friendship and a fine luncheon."

Fanshawe struck a pretentious pose and started to wail. Monk covered his ears.

Sigh no more, women, sigh no more,
Men are always lying;
One foot in sea, and one on land,
To one thing constant never.
Then sigh not so,
But let them go,
And be you blithe and happy,
Converting all your sounds of sadness
Into hey nappy, nappy.

Fanshawe's singing stopped abruptly and he looked around self-consciously. Jack realized what he was supposed to do and clapped heartily. "Well done!"

Angus joined in. "Er, very nice."

"A good effort, Harry," Trinculo said approvingly.

"Don't encourage him," Monk said. "It's taken him months to write that."

"You wrote it?" Jack said. "But . . ." Jack was confused. He had heard the song before—in fact he was sure it was from Shakespeare. It was from another play they had done—they had even watched a film of it in class—*Much Ado About Nothing*. So how could Fanshawe have written it?

"You say you wrote it? This is part of your work, and you say you have more?" Jack asked.

"You've done it now," Monk groaned.

But Fanshawe seemed to be delighted by the question.

"Of course, come, I must show you."

Fanshawe led Jack toward the wagon.

"This will interest you, my boy."

Jack got to his feet to follow Fanshawe. He briefly looked back at Angus, who shrugged his shoulders. Fanshawe climbed into the back of the wagon and Jack climbed after him. It was stuffed full of clothes, bedding, and other paraphernalia. It looked like it had been the Fanshawe Players' home, costume wardrobe, and kitchen for months. It smelled terrible.

"Over here."

They crawled toward the front of the wagon, where Fanshawe unearthed a small wooden chest from under a pile of clothes.

"Here we are."

He took a large brass key which hung around his neck and proceeded to insert it into a lock in front of the chest.

Fanshawe beamed at Jack triumphantly. "There! What do you think?"

Jack did not quite know what to make of it. It really did not seem to be anything special—just ream upon ream of ink-stained paper in a scrawly handwriting that was difficult to read.

"It's very nice . . . but I don't . . ."

Fanshawe interrupted, "Look, here is the first page."

Jack looked down at the piece of paper that Fanshawe held in his hands.

It read: MR. HARRY FANSHAWE'S COMEDIES, HISTORIES, AND TRAGEDIES.

Below this was a contents page entitled: "A Catalogue" and beneath this were a series of titles divided into three sections: Comedies, Histories, and Tragedies.

Jack's brow creased in concentration. The titles on the contents page were familiar. Then his heart missed a beat when he realized what he was looking at. In amazement, he whispered to himself, "It's Shakespeare."

Fanshawe was still beaming. "I'm sorry, my friend, it's what?"

Jack couldn't believe it. Fanshawe seemed to be in possession of an entire volume of Shakespeare's work . . . several years before Shakespeare wrote it and over thirty years before the plays were compiled into a single printed edition of his work—the famous First Folio. Beattie had told them all about it. Back in the twenty-first century, there were only two hundred or so First Folios in existence and they were extremely valuable, selling for six million dollars or more.

How could this possibly be in the hands of Fanshawe in the back of a moldy old cart in the middle of a forest?

"Did you write all this?"

Fanshawe beamed proudly. "Every last word."

"But . . ."

Jack could not understand it. Was it possible that this failed actor, Harry Fanshawe, leader of a failed troupe of players—now on his last throw of the dice to somehow link up with the great Christopher Marlowe in Cambridge to save his career, was possibly the author of Shakespeare's works?

Jack scanned the titles on the page. He had the benefit of a very quick mind, but he was certainly no expert on Shakespeare. He knew *Hamlet* of course, but he had only learned that because they were putting it on at school in a couple of weeks. But he didn't really know too much about the other plays, except what Miss Beattie had drilled into them in class. Nevertheless, as he scanned the titles in the contents page he realized that there was something wrong.

He recognized the titles as similar to Shakespeare's . . . but not quite. It was as if they were not right, somehow. The titles included:

Love's Labour's Not Quite Found
The Twenty-Two Gentlemen of Verona
The Big Storm
Much Ado About an Absence of Something
All's Well That Ends Much Improved
A Midsummer Night Among the Fairies
The Tragical Historie of Dave, Prince of Denmark

It was apparent from the titles that even if Fanshawe had spent a lifetime creating Shakespeare's work, he had perhaps not done it very well. It needed work. A lot of work.

"Incredible," Jack murmured.

"You're too kind." Fanshawe basked in what he thought was Jack's admiration—clearly this was not the adulation that he typically received from either Trinculo or especially Monk, whose patience with the Fanshawe enterprise was wearing thin.

"Do you think I could have a look inside one of the plays?"

"Certainly, sir. Which one would you like to see?"

"What about that one—*The Tragical Historie of* . . . er, *Dave, Prince of Denmark*?"

"Certainly, my latest and proudest achievement." Fanshawe rummaged and drew out a sheath of ink-blotted papers. "Here we are."

Jack thumbed through the pages to find what he was looking for—Act III, Scene I. Jack scanned down the page—he knew the words he was looking for by heart, so even in Fanshawe's unfortunate scrawl he should be able to spot them.

He muttered to himself, reading down the list of names, "Polonius, then the king, then Polonius . . . This should be it . . . and then . . . Dave?"

"Yes—David—one of the main characters in this tragedy."

"Not Hamlet."

Fanshawe nodded thoughtfully. "Well, Jack, certainly *Hamlet* has a certain ring to it. . . . Yes, you're right . . . Hamlet . . . I like it! In fact, you're right. *Dave* does not sound right at all! Let's make it Hamlet. Much more . . . *Danish*. Providential!"

Jack began reading the great soliloquy—one of the most famous passages in the English language. But they weren't the words he remembered or expected:

'To be, or not to be; ay, there's the point.
To die, to sleep, is that it? Yes—that's it;
No, to sleep, to dream. Ay, marry, and off we go . . .'

Jack could hardly bear to read on. It was complete rubbish. "It's gobbledygook."

"Yes, I agree," Fanshawe said. "I don't know what that word means, Jack, but I certainly agree with you—it is certainly one of my favorite passages . . . certainly gobbledygook."

Jack murmured, "It's Shakespeare, but not as we know it."

"Harry. Can I suggest a couple of changes . . . for example, why not try the following?"

Jack closed his eyes and recited the words that he knew so well:

'To be, or not to be: that is the question:
Whether 'tis nobler in the mind . . .'

Jack completed the famous speech, which he had rehearsed for the school play. Fanshawe looked at Jack with an expression of complete and utter awe.

"You have a gift—a gift of genius—a gift from heaven itself. How?"

Jack smiled. "Oh, I guess I'm a bit like you, Fanshawe—I have a knack with words."

Fanshawe's eyes were agape. "But that was truly incredible! You have talent, my boy . . . providential talent."

Jack blushed. He knew he probably should not have done it, but he just smiled and said, "Really, it's nothing."

But before Jack could say anything else, Angus stuck his head through the curtains at the rear of the wagon.

"You guys going to be long? 'Cause we got a problem. A big problem."

Bandit Country

There was something feral about the three men who stood in the path before them. Their faces and clothes, more like rags, were filthy. It was as if they had emerged from the undergrowth of the surrounding forest and were in some way part of it. Two of them brandished large wooden clubs, and a third a long knife. It was this third man who spoke through a toothless mouth.

"We don't want much," he said. "Just everything you've got."

Trinculo was shaking, and the bells on his hat started to tinkle.

"We have nothing," Fanshawe announced bravely, puffing out his chest.

But no sooner had the words come from Fanshawe's mouth than the ringleader wielded his great knife. It cut through the air and caught Fanshawe hard on the side of the thigh. Fanshawe wailed and collapsed to his knees, whimpering.

"We haven't time for this. Stave, search the cart. Butcher and me will see what this lot have on them." He immediately reached down to Fanshawe's neck and yanked off a thin silver chain and cross that hung there. "That'll do nicely, for a start."

Fanshawe sobbed louder.

Suddenly, Fanshawe's small wooden chest was thrown from the back of the cart and Stave jumped out after it.

"I found this."

He booted the chest, which flew open, and the precious papers that Fanshawe had shown Jack scattered across the muddy ground.

Fanshawe wailed hysterically.

The ringleader prodded him with his stick. "Shut your mouth— or you'll get more of this."

He strode over to the chest. "What is it?"

Trinculo and Monk were silent.

He turned back to them and snarled, "I asked what is it?"

Monk said quietly, "Plays, poems."

Trinculo mumbled, "They're not worth anything."

But the ringleader had a glint in his eye. "Not what I hear. You can get ten shillings for a play . . . maybe more, if it's any good."

The bandits gathered around the papers, suddenly interested.

Jack whispered to Angus from the side of his mouth, "Any ideas?"

"Tony and Gordon carried the only weapons, but I did manage to sneak this with me . . . was at the bottom of my schoolbag for some reason."

Angus opened his doublet fractionally for Jack to see what was inside. He had brought his catapult. And it wasn't a homemade one — Angus's had a slingshot of high-tensile industrial rubber tethered to a carbon-fiber frame. Jack seen Angus use this favorite toy to shatter a bottle over fifty feet away. He opened up the other side of his doublet.

"And I found a couple of these in the VIGIL prep area . . . pocketed them while the others weren't looking," he whispered.

A couple of tubes poked up from his inside pocket. Jack could not identify them.

"Thunder flashes," Angus said guiltily.

The bandits had become bored with the papers, which they hurriedly stuffed back into the wooden chest. The ringleader turned back to them.

"What else have you got?"

Angus reached into his pocket and pulled out one of the thin tubes and held it out.

"I have this. But I don't know if you will want it."

"What is it?"

Angus looked at Jack, who interjected, "We use it in our plays. . . . It is, er, a musical stick. It makes music."

"Loud music," Angus added.

The ringleader came closer. "I have never heard of such a thing. How does it work?"

"Easy," Angus said. "See that rock over there. Well, you just bang the bottom of the music stick on it and then hold it in your hand . . . and wait for the music."

Stave barged forward. "I want to do it!"

"No, me!" Butcher said.

"Stand aside. I will do it—I am the leader."

The ringleader took the thunder flash and marched over to the rock and manfully banged one end on the rock. "Like that?" he asked.

"Yes," replied Angus. "Just like that."

They waited.

The ringleader looked at them questioningly, "It's not work—"

Suddenly, there was a blinding flash of light and an earsplitting bang as the thunder flash went off in the hand of the bandit. For a second he was invisible in the swirling blue smoke, but as it cleared, he staggered blindly around, clutching his hand and wailing in pain.

His friends raced over to help him. Angus whipped out his catapult and selected a stone from the ground. In one movement he stretched back the rubber, extending it all the way from his arm to his earlobe. He closed his left eye and narrowed his right along the length of the rubber and . . . released. Jack could have sworn he heard the stone hiss angrily through the air. It caught Stave on his kneecap and he sank to the ground, emitting a low guttural grunt. Butcher turned, his face red with anger, and pelted toward them, wielding his club as he came. But Angus had coolly reloaded the catapult and unleashed a second shot. It was extraordinary that a small pebble could stop a grown man in his tracks. But it did. Angus had again skillfully targeted the leg, and now all three of their assailants were on the ground— alive, but in a great deal of pain.

Angus reloaded for a third time, but Jack put his hand up.

"I think we're done."

Angus lowered the catapult.

Fanshawe was on his feet and wrapped Angus and Jack in a bear hug. "Thank you, my friends."

Trinculo immediately performed another jig—just as embarrassing as the first.

Jack and Angus approached the three bandits, who groaned in the mud.

"Will they be OK?" Jack asked.

"Unfortunately, yes; they'll be limping around for a day or two . . . and what's-his-face will have a nasty burn on that hand . . . but they'll be fine."

Jack looked down at the three men. He wasn't quite sure what to say, but tried his best tough-man voice. "Come near us again . . . and, well . . . we've got a lot more tricks up our sleeves . . . and you'll regret it. We'll, er, be calling 911."

Angus tried not to smile. The bandits looked up at them with a mixture of confusion and fear. They seemed to have gotten the message.

They approached Cambridge from the northwest in the afternoon of the following day. They experienced no more trouble, but nevertheless the journey had been tough and progress painfully slow along the pitted roads. They had taken turns riding on the cart, but most of the time they had walked. Since their impromptu rabbit lunch, they had eaten very little—although Jack and Angus had, on occasion, dipped surreptitiously into their emergency rations. It was only because of this that they had managed to keep going, and Jack had no idea how the others were managing.

Despite little food, Fanshawe babbled incessantly. Subjects included their miraculous escape from the bandits, the details of which Fanshawe and Trinculo repeated again and again, each time their exploits becoming braver and more exaggerated, and the role of Angus, in particular, being raised to that of demigod. Even Monk added a grudging recognition of thanks. Then Fanshawe turned to his great plans for the future of the Fanshawe Players and how, working with the young genius that he had 'discovered'—one Jack Christie—they would all become famous and make their fortunes. Finally, he talked enthusiastically about their forthcoming meeting with Christopher Marlowe and their final destination, the town of Cambridge, or as he called it, "the most exquisite in all of Christendom."

Day of Deliverance

*   *   *

When they finally made it to Cambridge and crossed Magdalene Bridge, Jack got a sense of why Fanshawe had been so animated about the town. To his left, the red brick buildings of Magdalene College stretched gracefully out along the River Cam. To his right he set eyes upon a number of beautiful stone buildings and the spires of churches which rose gracefully above the rooftops. It was a stark contrast to the dirty hovels and huts that they had passed on their journey from Fotheringhay. They pressed on into the town and the crowds became thicker. It may have been a market day, as it was busy, and they frequently had to navigate past oncoming carts or gaggles of students, hawkers, or even monks. They turned right and passed Saint John's College and then Trinity College with its Great Court. As they progressed it was as if each building became bigger and grander. Finally, they reached King's College Chapel. It was a magnificent stone building, which towered almost a hundred feet into a gray sky, eclipsing everything else around it. At each corner stood a high tower, and there was a glorious stained-glass window built into the front elevation. Soon they were all gazing up in wonder at the great building, even the irascible Monk.

After a little while, they walked on, past the entrance to King's College, and finally Fanshawe announced, "We're here."

To his left Jack peered through an archway into the quad of yet another college. It was certainly not as large or as grand as the great colleges they had already passed, but it was still very beautiful. Opposite the arched gateway, Jack could see an elegant chapel set into the college buildings.

"Is this Corpus Christi College?"

"Yes, this is where we will meet my friends and where I have made arrangements for us to stay. You can make your way down to your lodgings at Queen's later. First things first, however; we must see to the cart and donkey."

As they got themselves organized, they were distracted by a group of young men who approached from farther down the street. They appeared to be in good humor and were singing loudly. They had been drinking. As they neared the college gate, Fanshawe approached one of the men, who had wavy auburn hair and wore a black cloak with large buttons. The man was young with a roundish, pale face and a light mustache and beard not unlike Fanshawe's. He was unsteady on his feet, and he put out one hand to steady himself on the college wall.

"May I help you, sir?" Fanshawe asked the man.

Fanshawe looked a little closer, peering into the man's face, his brow furrowed. "Marlowe? Christopher Marlowe?"

Marlowe looked back at Fanshawe, blinking and trying to focus his eyes. He let out a strange, strangled giggle, swayed again, and then he vomited profusely.

Corpus Conundrum

They were standing in the great wood-paneled hall of Corpus Christi College. Dinner had finished, and Marlowe's group of players had been permitted to clear the far end of the hall to complete an evening rehearsal of his new play, *Tamburlaine the Great.* The arrival of Jack, Angus, Fanshawe, Trinculo, and Monk had caused quite a stir among the players, and contrary to Monk's expectation, Fanshawe was well known to Marlowe and a number of his actors. They had been welcomed (particularly as there was a shortage of extra soldiers for the play). However, things were not going according to plan.

Marlowe himself, having thrown up at the college gates when they met, was now flat out on the floor at the far end of the hall, sleeping off a heavy afternoon in the Eagle pub. Meanwhile, the actor playing Mycetes, enemy of Tamburlaine, was rapidly following Marlowe into a comparable stupor, having discovered the key to the wine cellar beneath the hall. In addition, progress had been further delayed because Marlowe had insisted that in order to mark the occasion of the first public performance of *Tamburlaine,* he would arrange for a local artist to paint a portrait of the group. Prior to each rehearsal, the painter had lined up the entire cast in full costume and started scratching away at his easel. He was fussy and temperamental, and the arrival of Fanshawe, who insisted that they should also be in the picture, had nearly caused him to walk out. Reluctantly, he had been persuaded to stay, and the group stood posing appropriately, with Jack and Angus off to one side.

The actors had been standing for the painter for forty minutes and were getting bored and impatient to get on with the rehearsal. It had also become apparent that Mycetes had, in fact, smuggled an entire case of wine from the cellar, bottles from which were circulating happily around the group. As they did so the noise level increased and the behavior and language became increasingly coarse. When the first half-loaf of bread left over from dinner flew from one side of the hall to the other, rapidly followed in the opposite direction by a large lamb chop, Jack felt it was probably time to leave. He didn't want to be there when the College Master turned up to witness them in the middle of that most ancient of university traditions—the drunken food fight.

Jack nudged Angus. "Think it's time to move."

"Shame—just when it's getting interesting."

Jack turned to Fanshawe, who seemed to be the only one taking a rather dim view of the proceedings. "Harry, shouldn't we see how Marlowe is doing? Remember your plays—you wanted to show them to him?"

Fanshawe and the faithful Trinculo needed no excuse, and they slipped over to the far end of the hall where Marlowe lay, still snoring loudly. They woke him and he slowly regained his senses. He pulled himself to his feet and stood unsteadily, clutching his head and groaning.

"What happened?" he asked woozily. Then he saw the melee in the hall in front of them. Monk had compensated for living off starvation rations for weeks by satiating himself with food and wine and somehow had managed to suspend himself from the candelabra that hung from the vaulted ceiling. He swung gently to and fro, slurping from a bottle. The artist had packed his things and marched toward them in a furious temper, the unfinished canvas under one arm.

"I will send you the bill," he announced as he flounced past. Jack caught a glimpse of the unfinished painting as it swished before them, and on it he saw a preliminary outline of Fanshawe, Trinculo, Monk, Angus, and himself.

Marlowe groaned. "No chance of rehearsal now, I guess." A sudden look of concern washed over his face. "But come, we have more pressing business. We should retire to my rooms."

* * *

Day of Deliverance

Marlowe had acquired two adjoining rooms in the college, and the embers of a log fire still smoldered in the grate. Despite this, the room remained icily cold. Fanshawe immediately stoked up the fire and added a couple of logs. The room was a mess—papers and clothes were strewn everywhere. As Marlowe sobered up, it became increasingly apparent that he was nervous about something. When they had met that afternoon, he had been blind drunk and seemed not to have a care in the world, but he was very different now. On entering his rooms he had carefully locked the door behind them and peered furtively from the window onto the quad below. Next, he reached for a large bottle of brandy which sat before them on a small wooden table. Having only just recovered from one drinking bout, he nevertheless poured the brandy into a glass tumbler and drank the whole thing in one go before refilling his glass. He then reached for four more tumblers and filled them all to the brim. Jack remembered Beattie's translation of the text beneath Marlowe's portrait in her book:

What feeds me destroys me.

In fact he looked a little like the portrait. He had intelligent eyes, wavy brown hair, a round, somewhat pallid face, and a thin mustache and beard. Jack felt he should be in awe of the man who had so influenced the theater. But what surprised Jack was that Marlowe was so young, only twenty-three—scarcely eight years older than Jack. It was hard to think of him as a great literary figure. Jack remembered that in only four years Marlowe would be dead—killed in a brawl by a dagger stabbed into his head above the right eye. Many thought it was murder—or even an assassination—brought about by Marlowe's love of risk-taking and maybe his role as a spy or a double agent caught up in the dark world of Elizabethan espionage. Jack wondered whether he should inform the great man exactly how and when he would die and whether, in fact, this would accelerate or slow his creative output.

Promptly, Marlowe emptied his glass for a second time and leaned back in his chair and stared at the ceiling with an expression of deep concern. Suddenly his face changed, and he let out a strange, manic giggle—a bit like he had when they met him at the college gate. Clearly, the great Christopher Marlowe was slightly unhinged.

". . . and this is another of my favorites—a play about Scotland—it's called *Macgregor*." Fanshawe was trying to puncture Marlowe's pensive mood and interest him in his writing. He had brought his chest of papers up to the room to show Marlowe, hoping that he might generate sufficient enthusiasm to close a sale. Marlowe leafed through the papers, but he remained distracted.

"I am sure it is good work, Harry, but as you know, more work is the last thing I need at the moment. . . ." Again he giggled, and the noise sounded strangely out of place.

Fanshawe looked crestfallen.

But Marlowe remained untouched. "I am so busy with my own material . . . and we are just starting *Tamburlaine* . . ." He thought for a moment. "Although I do hear that there is a young writer in London, eagerly looking for new material. I may even proffer some of my own. He is ambitious and quite well-connected, I understand."

Fanshawe's eyes lit up. "London? What is the young man's name?"

"I am not sure I remember." Marlowe closed his eyes for a moment. "Shake-Shaft, I think; yes, that was it. Wilbur Shake-Shaft . . . I understand he frequents the Cross Keys Inn on Grace Church Street."

Suddenly Marlowe stopped talking and leaped to his feet. Jack had heard nothing, but Marlowe, in his heightened state of paranoia, seemed to be attuned to the smallest noise. He rushed over to the window and again peered out from behind the curtain.

He wheeled around. He had turned completely pale.

"They're here. They must have seen you. I feared this might happen."

He rushed over to a small desk on the opposite side of the room and frantically fiddled a key into the lock on a drawer. He opened it and rummaged inside. He pulled out a folded document sealed with red wax on one side. His hand shook as he held out the document.

"Fanshawe, we have been friends for a long time. You must help me. I beg you."

Jack and Angus looked at each other anxiously.

"What is—" Fanshawe started to speak, but Marlowe interjected, his words hurried.

"Guard this document with your life. You must take it to Walsingham—only he can see it. Do not open it. It is sealed—so he will know if it has been tampered with."

Fanshawe's eyes widened. "You want me to deliver this to Sir Francis Walsingham? But . . ."

"Yes, yes—Sir Francis Walsingham, the Queen's secretary—at court," Marlowe confirmed in frustration. "It is of national importance. If they find it here with me they will suspect me and surely kill me. . . ."

"But—"

"Do not question me. No one will know that you have it. Go now and you will be safe—and if it is put securely into Walsingham's hand, he will reward you handsomely." Marlowe reached into a pocket and took out a small velvet bag. "For your trouble. Gold—take it."

They heard the sound of heavy boots tramping up the stairs, and despite the temperature of the room, Jack saw small beads of sweat materializing on Marlowe's forehead. He looked around desperately.

"I know!"

He led them into the small adjoining bedroom and opened a window. The cold winter air rushed in.

"Go out here—the college roof is just up there. You can make your way down on the other side. Don't worry; it's easy and it will be quiet. You have more than enough there to get you to London safely—and then to Walsingham."

"But what about my work?" Fanshawe said, looking at the chest of papers which still lay beside the table.

Angus rolled his eyes and started to snatch the papers from Fanshawe's chest. "Here—stuff them in our backpacks. We'll take what we can. . . . Come on."

Jack started to help Angus while Fanshawe worried about the papers getting torn or damaged.

"Stop fussing—we don't have time," Angus hissed.

Suddenly there was a thunderous bang on the door, and a heavily accented voice called out. "Marlowe, who is there? Are you safe?"

Marlowe was already bundling Fanshawe and Trinculo through the window. There was a loud bang as a firearm discharged right outside Marlowe's door.

"That was a gun—I'm not hanging around any longer." Angus jumped out through the window, hot on the heels of Fanshawe and Trinculo.

Marlowe passed back into the main room as Jack climbed up onto the windowsill, following the others. Ahead, Jack could just see Angus's frame silhouetted against the light of the moon as he scrambled up from Marlowe's window and onto the roof of the college. Jack glanced back over his shoulder into the main room. As he did, the door flew open. For the last time Jack heard Marlowe's nervous giggle, but did not wait to see his fate. He turned and fled through the window and into the night.

Night Climb

They raced across the roof of Corpus Christi College. A full moon washed the chimneys and crenulations in a shadowy monochrome. Jack's eyes adjusted quickly—he could soon see well enough to be sure of his footing and of the position of the others ahead of him.

"This way!"

Angus waved them forward, and Jack saw him clamber up and over a wall that abutted the far end of the college roof. A secured ladder led down to another roof below, and Fanshawe and Trinculo followed Angus down obediently. Jack paused to catch his breath. Behind, he could still see the yellow glow of candlelight from Marlowe's rooms. Suddenly, he saw a figure clamber out of the window and up onto the roof, just as Jack and the others had done minutes before. He was quickly followed by a second figure—squatter, but powerfully built. They were being followed—presumably by the people who had shot through Marlowe's door. Jack couldn't figure it out. They had not seen Jack and the others escape to the roof, so Marlowe must have shown the men where they had gone. Why on earth would he do that?

Jack crouched down low. Although the roof was long and the men were still about a hundred and fifty feet away, there was little cover, and the light of the moon silhouetted Jack against the low-rise wall that edged the roof. The first man was now straddling the apex of the roof with a foot on each side. He stopped and appeared to reach for something strapped to his back. In the poor light, Jack could not see what it was, but the man brought the object forward and then up to his eye and pointed it directly at Jack. There was a loud *thwack* and almost instantaneously a small chunk of masonry dislodged from the wall behind Jack. A metal object rebounded from the brickwork and then clattered back onto the slating and rolled down toward the guttering. It was a crossbow bolt—and Jack was being used for early evening target practice.

Jack immediately clambered over the wall and down the ladder to the lower roof, following the others. He could see that they had already made it down to the street, and from below Angus waved him toward a heavy drainpipe. Jack scraped and slipped down the wall, using the drainpipe for support, and finally reached the street. He felt as if his head were going to burst.

"Can't stay here." He panted and waved up toward the roof line. "We've got trouble. Those men are following us from Marlowe's rooms. I've no idea what's going on but he must have told them about us. They've got guns and crossbows."

"Who are they? What do they want?" Fanshawe whimpered.

"They're trouble, Harry, just like your 'friend' Marlowe. He's got us into something, and I don't want to hang around to find out what," Trinculo said.

"Let's go toward the town center . . . probably safest if we can find a crowd," Jack said.

Just then, the air above them hissed and a second crossbow bolt embedded itself in the side of a wooden cart parked against the college wall.

Turning from the side street, they raced back past the entrance to Corpus Christi and toward the great towers of King's College Chapel, which loomed into view on their left. There seemed to be quite a gathering of people at the college gate, and they could hear the choir singing in the chapel not far beyond.

Jack spotted their chance. "Mix in with these people going to the chapel. There must be a service or something."

They slowed to a brisk walk as they joined the crowd, so as not to stand out. Soon they were through the gatehouse and walking across the quad toward the entrance of the vast Gothic chapel, their path guided by lanterns burning on each side of the path. Jack looked behind. It was difficult to see clearly since there was quite a line of people—but then, coming out of the gatehouse about thirty feet behind them, he was sure he recognized the shapes of their two pursuers. Jack felt a burning urge to break and sprint away from the crowd, which slowed as it approached the chapel. He knew if he did, the men would be on to them immediately. There was safety in the group of people that inched its way agonizingly toward the chapel, which soared into the night sky like some vast ship.

At last, they were inside. The great chapel was only lit by the gentle flicker of candles, but even by this light Jack could see that the building was magnificent—a huge rectangular cavern with clifflike walls and windows soaring up to a spectacular fan-vaulted ceiling way, way above.

Angus elbowed him in the ribs. "Wake up. What now?"

People were gradually taking seats for the service. They had minutes at most before their pursuers followed them inside the chapel.

"What about over there?" Angus whispered. He pointed to a small wooden door set into the wall in the near corner of the chapel.

"Worth a try, but don't get noticed."

They moved quietly over to the door, aided by the shadows inside the chapel. While the others formed a screen, Jack tried the handle.

"It's open!"

He eased the door ajar and, checking that no one was watching, they all slipped into what seemed to be a large, dark closet. Except it couldn't be a closet, because gray moonlight glimmered through a narrow window above them.

"What is this place?" Angus whispered.

"It's the bottom of one of the chapel turrets. Look, there are stairs," Fanshawe replied.

"Do you think anyone saw us?"

"I don't know; it was pretty dark in there, but we don't want to risk it. Let's go."

Jack started to climb the narrow spiral staircase. After a few minutes they reached a second wooden door, which opened onto the massive roof of the chapel. The turret was one of the twin turrets at the west end of the chapel that looked out over the river Cam. On the opposite side of the roof soared the taller twin turrets built into each corner of the east end of the chapel. They stood in silence in the doorway at the top of the spiral staircase, straining for any sound from below.

"Hear anything?"

The choir had stopped singing and the congregation below was still, awaiting the start of the service. Suddenly, they heard a scrape of ghostly footsteps echoing up the spiral staircase toward them.

"They're coming!" Angus whispered, panic in his voice. "We can't go back down there, and there's no way off this roof."

"The other turrets?" Jack said. "They must have staircases, too! We could go back down in one of them."

Angus smiled. "Nice one."

The four of them dashed across the roof toward the turrets on the east side. Angus rattled the door handle of the northeast tower.

"It's locked!"

"So, try that one." Jack pointed at the southeast turret, and they clambered up over the crest of the roof and down toward it. It was a cold night, but Jack's palms were sticky with sweat. He turned the handle of the door to the southeast turret.

"Locked, too."

"Crap," Angus said between his teeth. "Those guys will be up on the roof in no time. We're trapped."

"I don't want a crossbow bolt in my head," Fanshawe said, trembling.

"Unless . . ." Angus craned up at the massive octagonal turret that towered above them, tapering into the darkness of the night sky.

"No way," Jack said.

"We don't have a choice. I don't want to be around when those guys get here. I think it looks quite easy, actually—all those vent holes and gargoyles or whatever they are should help. We don't need to go all the way up—just to that parapet thing in the shadows so they can't see us."

Fanshawe was shaking.

Jack took a deep breath and turned to Fanshawe and Trinculo. "OK, then. Let's go. The crest of the roof should give us some cover for a few minutes as we climb."

"But . . ."

Jack was frightened, but he felt himself getting angry. "Get a grip, Harry, or we're all dead. Do exactly what Angus does . . . and don't look down."

Angus stepped from the roof balustrade and up onto a sloping slab of stone a few feet up the turret.

"It's not bad—the stone is quite grippy," he whispered down.

Fanshawe, Trinculo, and then Jack started to follow Angus up the outside of the turret—placing their hands and feet in exactly the same positions that Angus did. They were pumped up with adrenaline, and their progress was surprisingly quick. After a few feet, Angus came to his first obstacle—a large stone overhang. By stretching his hand over the overhang he located a cloverleaf air hole, which gave him just enough purchase to lever himself up and over. He rapidly ascended the next section until he arrived at a further overhang at the bottom of the parapet. He repeated the maneuver and suddenly found himself inside the stone parapet—a sort of decorative crown a good fifty feet above roof level. From here, he was able to lean over and help first Fanshawe, then Trinculo, and finally Jack up and into the parapet.

They just made it in time. Looking across the roof from their position perched up in the shadows, they saw two figures emerge from across the roof.

"Keep down!" Jack whispered.

They crouched behind the low crenulated wall of the parapet. Fanshawe was exhausted and moved to sit down in the narrow gap inside the parapet. Jack wish he hadn't—there was a loud squawk as a fat pigeon made a brave bid for freedom from Fanshawe's descending buttocks. But Fanshawe was unable to stop his downward momentum, and the poor bird was flattened.

"Don't move!" Angus hissed.

Below, the two men cautiously approached the eastern turrets, their crossbows at the ready. They tested the locked doors of each of the eastern turrets in turn. Jack could hear them in furtive discussion, and he strained to hear what they were saying. All he could tell was that they were not speaking English. It sounded more like Italian or Spanish.

After a further search of the roof, the men crept back over to the open doorway in the northwest tower and melted back into the staircase. Jack leaned his head on the stonework behind him and let out a long sigh of relief.

Angus whispered, "They've gone. What now?"

"We can't stay up here—we'll freeze to death."

"We should stay here for as long as we can stand it, then drop back down—maybe when the service is finishing."

Angus peered down. "Think it's going to be harder getting down than coming up." He thought for a moment. "I know—give me that."

He took his own backpack, and then Jack's, and fiddled with the straps to tie them together. "Not perfect, but I can probably use this to sort of belay each of you down . . . at least over the overhang so you can get a foothold."

When they saw people beginning to leave the chapel, they started their descent. Jack went first—initially dangling like a pendulum from the straps of the backpack. For a moment he was just hanging in space two hundred feet above the street below. If Angus let go or if he slipped, he would have three seconds alive. At last, his foot touched the safety of one of the cloverleaf air holes, and in a few minutes he had picked his way back down to the safety of the roof. The others followed, and soon they were back at the open tower door. All was quiet. Then, as they started their way back down the spiral staircase, Jack noticed another small wooden door—one they had not seen on their way up.

"Hey, what's this?" He tried the handle. "This is open. Come on!" There was no light, but regardless, they pressed in and closed the door behind them. They were in the giant attic area of King's Chapel between the roof and above the great stone fan-vaulting. The thin layer of stone under their feet was the only thing between them and the vast emptiness of the chapel below.

"It's musty in here."

"But we're inside and safe. I vote we hunker down here till morning and then make our move."

Jack awoke shivering. His whole body ached. The nervous exhaustion from their efforts the night before had somehow allowed them a night of fitful sleep on the stone floor. There was now some light in the attic area, and he reached over and gently shook the huddled shapes of the others, who awoke groaning.

They retraced their footsteps down the spiral staircase and then crept out the door at the bottom of the turret and into the chapel. Soon they were across the quad and through the college gate and onto the street. Jack was tired, cold, and aching, but he was also exhilarated by their incredible escape. He banged Angus on the back.

"We made it!"

Suddenly, he felt a cold lump of metal pressing against the back of his neck.

A voice whispered, "Do exactly what I say."

Peace, Love, and Understanding

They were bundled into a covered cart. One of their assailants jumped into the back of the cart with them while the other took the reins at the front. Jack had little time to study the men, but he could tell immediately they were not the Spaniards who had pursued them up onto the chapel roof the night before.

The man with the pistol was firm but surprisingly polite. "I apologize for the rough tactics, but you are in great danger. I would like you each to lie down on the bottom of the cart until we get out of town. We will then have more time to explain."

"But—" Trinculo started to complain. But the man thrust the pistol into his face, suddenly flushed with anger.

"Do what I say," he ordered.

They lay flat on the rough wooden surface of the cart. Although Jack was scared, he noticed that those were some very modern handguns their captors were wielding.

Jack's body was still aching from the night spent up in the tower, and the aching was immediately made worse by his being banged around on the bottom of the cart as they headed out of town. After a while, the driver turned back toward his colleague.

"Here, this'll do."

The cart rumbled to a halt.

"OK, gentlemen. I want you to get up, one by one, and step down from the cart. Please don't try anything stupid."

They had pulled over by some trees next to the road. The landscape was flat and boggy for miles in every direction, and in the distance they could still see the spires of Cambridge. The sun had come up into a clear blue winter sky, and Jack waited for its weak rays to warm him up.

"Sit down by the wall there."

The men seemed to have become more relaxed now that they were out of Cambridge. They both looked to be in their midthirties, fit, and clean-shaven.

"Here we go."

The taller of the two men handed them a steaming thermos. Fanshawe and Trinculo looked confused.

"What is it?"

The man chuckled. "Not something you will have tasted. We call it tea."

Jack took a sip. As the hot liquid slipped down his throat he began to feel warmer.

"And this might help . . ."

The man handed out some dried salted beef. Again, Fanshawe and Trinculo were suspicious, but seeing Angus and Jack help themselves, they joined in.

"Better?" the man said. Jack nodded. "First—an apology for the gun-toting. We needed to get you out of there quickly. Now . . . introductions."

"My name is James Whitsun"—he gestured to the shorter man—"and my colleague here is Tim Gift."

But Jack had already figured out who they were. "You're Revisionists."

Gift smiled. "And of course you are the famous Jack Christie and Angus Jud." He sighed. "You don't know how much trouble you've caused us."

"So can you explain who those people are who were trying to kill us and what is going on?"

Whitsun took a slug of tea and a deep breath. "Yes. Your friend Marlowe does not just write plays. He has some unusual, and dangerous, friends. He also has an addiction to risk-taking . . . and money. He seems to have gotten himself into a position where he is what we would call a double agent. He works for the English state, but he also works for the Spanish state. Not a particularly comfortable position to be in, since there is virtually a war going on between them . . . but he thinks he's cleverer than both."

"Those people that chased us last night . . . they were Spanish?"

"Correct, Jack. Marlowe is involved in a Spanish plot against the English state. Those men that chased you last night are Spanish agents who are working with Marlowe. Marlowe has all sorts of connections among the aristocracy and the court, so he is a useful asset. The Spanish are known to us, and we have, er, inveigled our way into their trust. Recently, however, Marlowe has also come to the attention of Sir Francis Walsingham—Secretary of State."

"More or less the founder of England's first secret service," Gift added.

"The Spaniards have been keeping a close eye on Marlowe and saw you accompany him to his rooms. They were suspicious that you were working for Walsingham and might be after Marlowe. In order to save himself, we understand that Marlowe said that you had threatened him and had searched his apartment, but had panicked when the Spaniards arrived. He said that you then escaped with knowledge of the plot to take to Walsingham in London."

"And they believed that?"

"Marlowe got away with it—he is no fool—and the Spanish will have him safe and secure by now. He betrayed you, and you have been very lucky. When we became aware of what had happened, we were able to distract the Spaniards sufficiently to pick you up."

Fanshawe muttered bitterly, "If I ever see that Marlowe again, I'll . . ."

Jack interrupted, "So, how do you know these Spanish guys? What do you mean, they trust you? And how did you find us?"

Whitsun glanced nervously at Fanshawe and Trinculo. "That's a little too much information for just now, Jack. However, we are going to take you somewhere safe and to someone who can answer all your questions."

"Who?" Angus said.

"Dr. Pendelshape, of course."

Jack's heart skipped a beat when he heard the name.

"But first, we need to know—did Marlowe give you anything before he left?"

Fanshawe looked nervously at Jack. Jack nodded. "Tell them, Harry."

"A letter—I swore on my life not to open it—and money for our services to take it to Walsingham," Fanshawe replied.

"Perfect. If you can hand us the letter, please."

Fanshawe hesitated.

"Please," Whitsun insisted, an undercurrent of menace in his voice.

Fanshawe reached into an inside pocket and handed the letter to Whitsun, who whisked it away from him. "Very good. We certainly don't want this getting into the wrong hands."

Gift got to his feet. "And now I'm afraid we have some rather unpleasant business to see to." He removed his pistol from inside his cloak and eyed Fanshawe and Trinculo menacingly.

"Jack, Angus, you may want to look away. . . . This is necessary business, I'm afraid, but not pleasant."

Jack was incredulous. "Hold on, you're not going to—"

"Don't intervene, Jack. These people already know far too much—their knowledge could wreck our plans . . ."

As Gift spoke, he noticed an odd figure approaching from the town a little way down the path. He was perched upon a donkey and wore a gray hooded cloak like a friar from a monastery. As he approached their group, he dismounted and led the donkey toward them.

As the man walked toward them, Gift surreptitiously reholstered his weapon.

"What now?" he muttered impatiently.

The figure walked slowly, his cloaked head pointed modestly toward the ground. He did not reveal his face.

"What do you want, old man?" Gift said.

"Alms for the poor."

"We have nothing—go away," Whitsun replied in frustration, "We're busy."

"In that case, peace be with you."

Still without raising his head, the friar did a sign of the cross in the air. Then, as Whitsun and Gift started to turn away disinterestedly, the friar placed his hand inside his cloak and withdrew a heavy wooden club. The first blow caught Gift square on the head, and he crumpled to the ground. Whitsun reached for his weapon, but he was not quick enough. With his second blow, the friar buried the club in Whitsun's face. Whitsun fell to his knees clutching his nose. The friar landed a second blow to Whitsun's head, and he too fell unconscious to the ground.

"As I said, peace be with you, brothers . . ."

The friar threw back his hood, and his face was revealed.

"Monk!" Fanshawe cried. Immediately Fanshawe and Trinculo embraced their old friend.

"Steady, steady."

"But how . . . ?"

"You didn't think I would let the great Fanshawe Players leave town without me, did you?"

"You followed us?"

"We were thrown out of the college late last night. I checked Marlowe's rooms, but he was gone . . . and so were you. I searched the whole college, but there was no trace of any of you. I had to sleep in one of the staircases. This morning, I saw you come out of King's College. I was about to shout, and then I saw those two men take you. I decided to follow . . ."

They laughed. "Thank you for that, Monk. I didn't know you cared . . ."

Monk shrugged sheepishly. "You're the only family I have."

Jack knelt down to inspect Whitsun and Gift.

"Are they dead?" Angus asked.

Jack felt for their pulses. "No, but they're down for the count."

"What do we do?"

Jack thought to himself. "They can take us to Pendelshape, but on the other hand, they are completely ruthless—look what they just tried to do."

Monk wielded his club. "I say we finish them off right now."

Jack put up his hand. "No. You don't want blood on your hands. We tie them up good and well and that'll give us time to leave. Angus, you help me search them and we'll take anything useful."

In a minute, Jack and Angus were rummaging through the clothes and belongings of the two men while Fanshawe, Trinculo, and Monk prepared to leave.

Angus removed the two pistols. "We'll take those, for a start."

"And I think we'll take Marlowe's letter back," Jack said.

Suddenly Jack felt a smooth object in one of the inside pockets.

He looked around to ensure the others were busy. "Hey, Angus," he whispered, "how much do you think VIGIL would like to get hold of a Revisionist time phone?"

Angus smiled slyly, revealing an object he had just recovered from Whitsun.

"Or even two Revisionist time phones."

The Cross Keys

Jack felt like he could smell all 200,000 people who were bundled together into 400 acres of narrow, fetid streets, slippery with the slime of rubbish. As they walked on, timber and plaster houses rose above them—their upper levels projected over the lower so that they almost met those on the opposite side of the street at the top. Periodically, refuse was thrown from the windows straight into the gloomy, sunless streets below. You had to take care to avoid a direct hit. In some places the streets were little better than open sewers. Fanshawe explained that the law had little pity on the residents, who were targeted by swindlers, pickpockets, cutpurses, cozeners, and countless other forms of lowlife. If the undesirables didn't get you, disease probably would. The place was racked with it—bubonic plague, tuberculosis, measles, rickets, scurvy, smallpox, and dysentery. Yet, despite all this, there was nothing to match it in England or even Europe. This was a city destined to be the center of the largest empire the world had ever seen. A city that was vibrant, bustling, and dangerous—London.

With the money given to him by Marlowe for safe passage of the secret letter, Fanshawe rented a room at the *Cross Keys Inn* on Grace Church Street between Bishopsgate and London Bridge. The inn was built around a cobbled courtyard accessed through an archway from the street. Above the courtyard open balconies ran around the perimeter of each floor, and from here guests could watch plays put on from time to time by itinerant acting troupes. It did seem possible, therefore, that this was a good place to find Marlowe's contact, "Wilbur Shake-Shaft," but so far he had proved elusive.

Fanshawe, Trinculo, and Monk approached the bar to order lunch, leaving Jack and Angus at one of the wooden tables in a corner of the Cross Keys. Nearby, a log fire was spluttering to life, adding smoke but so far little warmth to the dank air. They had the table to themselves, and Jack and Angus took the chance to review their position without the others there.

Though neither Jack nor Angus could get used to the smell, one thing that they were getting used to was that nobody drank water because this risked illness. Ale was the next best thing. It was mostly weak but there were stronger brews. That morning, Fanshawe had thought nothing of downing two pints of Mad Dog at breakfast—a cloudy liquid with no froth. If you didn't like Mad Dog, you could try Huffcap, Merry-Go-Down, or Dragon's Milk. Or if you were feeling brave, Go-by-the-Wall or Stride Wide. Not wishing to die of thirst, Jack and Angus had little choice but to partake. Mad Dog was certainly an acquired taste, and it was all Jack could do not to retch as the liquid hit the back of his throat. Angus, with his larger frame, coped with the effects better. After half a pint, Jack's head was spinning.

"Well?" Jack nodded down at Angus's doublet, under which he had secreted his time phone.

"Dead as a dodo," Angus replied.

The time phones remained lifeless. There was still no communication from VIGIL or, for that matter, from Tony and Gordon, for whom they were beginning to fear the worst.

"What about the Revisionist time phones?"

"They've got the same problem as VIGIL—intermittent time signals. We have no choice but to wait. We have no other information to go on—we have to wait for a time signal so we can contact VIGIL."

Angus groaned. "We can't communicate with VIGIL, there's no sign of Tony and Gordon, but if we could get these Revisionist time phones to VIGIL—they would be able to infiltrate the Revisionists and blow their whole operation apart."

"And in the meantime, we're none the wiser about what the Revisionists are really up to. All we know is that it must have something to do with this Spanish plot and that letter to Walsingham," Jack added.

"Should we open it?"

"Yeah, I'm thinking it's about time we should. But bear in mind that if we do that, you know, break the seal, then Walsingham might just dismiss it—that's what Marlowe said, anyway."

"Well, at least we've bought some time—you know, with Whitsun and Gift out of the picture." Angus stared down at the table. "Do you think we should have . . ."

"What?" Jack asked.

"You know—taken care of business."

"I'll pretend you didn't say that, Angus. They might be murderers— but we're not. We've got their time phones, at least . . ."

"And we've got their guns."

"Yes, but Pendelshape is still at large—and maybe there are other Revisionists with him."

Angus glanced over at the bar where Fanshawe, Trinculo, and Monk were in an animated conversation with the owner about their lunch.

"What must they think?"

"They seem just happy to be alive."

"Excuse me." Their conversation was interrupted by a young man who stood at the end of their table. He had an accent that Jack could not place. He was dressed in a leather jerkin over a coarse shirt, with long breeches tucked into stiff leather boots. He had a mane of long, black curly hair and carried a bag full of papers over his shoulder. In one arm he cradled two large books.

"I was left a message that a Mr. Fanshawe was keen to meet and would wait at this table between the hours of eleven and three." He peered at them with dark, glinting eyes. "Is either of you Mr. Fanshawe?"

"No," Jack replied, "but here he comes now." Jack pointed over to where Fanshawe, Trinculo, and Monk were navigating their way through the growing lunchtime crowd back to the table, trying not to spill several large pewter tankards of ale. As they arrived, the man held out his hand.

"Mr. Harold Fanshawe?"

"Yes."

"I believe you wished to meet me . . . to do business. My name is Shakespeare. William Shakespeare."

A Bargain with the Bard

Fanshawe was well into his sales pitch and papers were strewn all over the table in front of them. Unlike Marlowe, Shakespeare appeared to be quite interested in Fanshawe's work. He must have been desperate. Maybe it made sense; the great man was still unknown and his fame lay many years ahead. He was looking for anything that might give him a start, an edge. Shakespeare had a nervous energy about him and flicked quickly from page to page. Occasionally he would look up and scratch his beard and make a comment like, "It will need work," or "This must change," or "This is wrong."

Fanshawe looked increasingly worried. Finally, he could take no more.

"What say you I read you something . . . bring the words to life?" He leafed through the papers in front of him, trying to locate a suitable passage.

"Here!" Fanshawe suddenly leaped to his feet, posed pretentiously and started to speak.

As Fanshawe read out the words, Shakespeare fidgeted with his beard and stifled a yawn. Jack cringed. Fanshawe's prose was truly dreadful and Jack could sense that, like Marlowe before him, Shakespeare was about to reject the work out of hand. Fanshawe's world was about to implode, and with it his fantasies of future wealth and fame. But then, much to Jack's surprise, Shakespeare gestured impatiently for Fanshawe to pass him the sheet from which he read. Fanshawe stopped abruptly and sat down, deflated. Shakespeare took the paper and pulled a quill and a small pot of ink from his bag, which he placed in front of him on the table. He opened the pot, dabbed the quill, and scribbled, murmuring to himself.

"This is wrong . . . and this . . . and this would be better here I think."

After a couple of minutes he had finished and beamed at them.

"Now, Harry, let me see if I understand what you were trying to say."

Shakespeare read out his revised version of Fanshawe's script:

Tomorrow, and tomorrow, and tomorrow,
Creeps in this petty pace from day to day . . .

He continued to read, and after a while he paused and looked up from the reworked script. "What do you think?"

Fanshawe stared at Shakespeare in awe. In just two minutes Shakespeare had transformed Fanshawe's efforts. Shakespeare turned to the play's title page: *Macgregor.*

With one final flourish of the quill he struck a line through *Macgregor,* and replaced it with *Macbeth,* and declared, "Better, I think. Also a real Scottish king."

"Yes, sir, much better—more . . . Scottish. You have a gift, sir," Fanshawe said in wonder.

"Yes, I know," Shakespeare replied. "But I usually need something to get me going. A starting point, if you like."

He took a long draft from one of the untouched tankards of ale, thumped it back onto the table, and declared, "I'll give you three pounds for the lot."

Fanshawe grimaced. He was hoping for more, but judging from the amount of rework that Shakespeare would need to do, this was a good offer, and Fanshawe was unlikely to do any better.

"Well, sir, I'm not sure . . ."

Jack cut in. "I don't want to be rude, Harry, but I think Mr. Shakespeare is making a good offer . . . as a, er, friend, I think you will do no better." Then Jack added with a twinkle in his eye, "I assure you—your work could not be in better hands."

With Jack's endorsement, Fanshawe relented and thrust out his hand.

"Three pounds it is, sir!"

"Good. Let's drink to that."

Jack and Angus watched as Fanshawe's papers passed from one side of the table to the other and were stuffed unceremoniously into Shakespeare's bag. Observing this transaction, Jack realized that they had unraveled one of the biggest mysteries of literary history: had Shakespeare himself written all of his own material, and if not, who had? Jack knew Fanshawe's work would give Shakespeare little advantage. But as the great man had said, it was a start.

Lunch arrived. Compensating for their meager rations over the last weeks, Fanshawe and Trinculo had ordered a vast array of food— meats, cheeses, cakes, and sweet pastries—all of which were delivered together. Lubricated by the arrival of wine and more ale, the conversation turned to the theatrical scene in London.

". . . and Henslowe has built a new theater, south of the river. The Rose."

"You know Henslowe?" Trinculo asked, glancing knowingly at Fanshawe.

"Of course. I was planning to pay a visit this afternoon."

Fanshawe seized his opportunity. "But William, as you know, we are looking for work. We have many years as players . . . and young Jack here has a fine talent, too. Maybe you could put a good word in for us with this Mr. Henslowe."

Shakespeare smiled. "I don't see why not. We can all pay him a visit." He looked at them mischievously. "And after that I have an excellent idea of how we may celebrate the completion of our business."

They turned south down Grace Church Street. Fanshawe, Trinculo, Monk, and Shakespeare were worse for the wear following their enormous lunch. Progress was further hindered by the appalling traffic. Carts pulled by two, four, or even six horses moved up and down the street (thankfully, this one was paved), and people wove in and out as best they could. As far as Jack could see there were no traffic rules, like "stay to the left" or "stop at intersections"—you just moved along as best you could. From the top of Fish Street they caught their first glimpse of the river—a broad expanse of gray-brown water much wider than in modern times. If anything, the river was even busier than the streets, with small sailing ships, rowboats, wherries, and decorated barges. The boats moved both up and down the river and to and fro across it because there was only one way to cross on foot—London Bridge.

Initially, Jack had the impression that they were going to cross over the famous structure, but as they drew closer he saw that it was congested by an entire flock of sheep emerging from its north end. Instead, they walked down steps to the water's edge where watermen touted for business. Fanshawe pushed forward and soon all six of them were packed precariously into a two-man wherry and were being rowed out into the icy current.

From their vantage point on the river they had an excellent view of the bridge with its twenty stone arches. A waterwheel had been built into the northernmost arch. On top of the arches, houses were built up to six stories high. Some projected far out over the river, balancing perilously on a system of struts and supports. Teetering at the southern end there was even a palace—Nonsuch House—complete with turrets and gilded columns and carved galleries. On the far side of the bridge you could make out the high masts of merchant ships waiting to unload at the Custom House.

As they approached the south side of the river, Jack spotted a number of long poles that projected high above a building on the southern end of the bridge. They had strange-looking blobs on the end, so they looked like giant matchsticks. For a while, Jack could not make out what they were, and then he understood. They were heads on top of the poles—the heads of traitors or serious criminals. They were a gruesome warning to all who passed beneath and a brutal reminder to Jack and Angus of the reality of the age in which they were stranded.

From the outside the Rose, in the Liberty district of Southwark, was a high polygonal structure of timber and plaster—it looked similar to the pictures of the Globe theater Jack had seen in books. The place seemed dead, but Fanshawe banged on the door anyway. There was silence. Fanshawe hammered on the door again and shouted, "Anyone at home?"

A voice replied from inside the building, "We're closed."

"We want to speak to Henslowe."

"He's busy."

They looked at one another.

Shakespeare spoke. "But we have urgent business with him."

"I told you he's very busy."

"Where is he?"

"At the pub."

Fanshawe rolled his eyes. "This is hopeless—maybe we should come back later."

Shakespeare's eyes twinkled. "Good idea." He nodded toward a group of people gathering nearby. "I know exactly how we can while away a few hours."

Quite close by there was a second building, larger than the Rose. Outside, a large and excited crowd jostled for position. Shakespeare, Fanshawe, and Trinculo pushed in, and Jack and Angus followed.

"What's all this?" Angus asked, his face pink with the cold.

"No idea," Jack replied.

Fanshawe paid two pennies for each of them to enter the building, and they found themselves standing in a large roofed gallery overlooking a large pit. The place was packed. It was as if there was a giant party going on. People were drinking and eating and there were occasional catcalls and loud whoops of excitement. The arena below looked a bit like a circus ring, but there was no evidence as to what form the entertainment would take. They didn't have to wait long to find out.

First of all, a horse was released into the arena. A waistcoated monkey clung on to its back and screeched loudly. Then, four small dogs were released from pens in the perimeter of the pit, and they started to chase the horse around and around the arena, snapping wildly at its hooves and jumping up at the monkey. The audience wailed with laughter. But Jack could see that the horse was terrified. Occasionally, a dog would manage to clamp its jaws around one of its legs, and the poor beast would buck wildly. The monkey would give an ear-piercing screech and hold on even more tightly to avoid toppling off. The horse bucked and kicked again and again until the dog was finally thrown free, whereupon the whole brutal procedure repeated itself. It was a sickening sight, but this was just the beginning.

After several circuits of the arena, the snapping dogs were pulled off and the bloodied horse led away. The mood in the crowd changed to a low chatter of anticipation. Suddenly, there was a crescendo of excitement and people pointed over to one side of the arena. A large bear was being led forward by two keepers. The great beast moved slowly and seemed to take little interest in the proceedings. The keepers kept prodding it with large sticks to drive it on. The bear was tethered by a chain attached to a manacle around one leg to a short post buried in the middle of the arena. The keepers moved off and for a moment the bear was left to sit quietly, minding its own business. Next a bull was released into the arena. Unlike the bear, it was highly agitated and circled the bear, hoofing the ground and tossing its head. Finally, four large mastiffs were released and, to the crowd's delight, complete mayhem ensued.

The hungry dogs attacked the bull first. Immediately one of them was speared by its horns and tossed high up into the air. It landed and did not move. This did not seem to put off the other mastiffs, which circled the bull, occasionally charging and snapping at its legs. Astonishingly, the keepers remained in the ring while the appalling spectacle played out. When the action seemed to subside they would prod one of the dogs with a stick and it would reenter the fray. After a while, the dogs became less interested in the bull, which was proving a highly resilient adversary, and turned their attention to the bear. They moved toward it, growling and getting closer and closer as they became braver. The mood of the bear transformed. It jumped up onto its hind legs, pawing at the dogs and roaring. Suddenly one of the mastiffs came in too close, snapping away with its razor sharp teeth. The bear got lucky. It grabbed the dog around its trunk and crushed it in a hug on its chest before discarding it like a rag doll.

Jack had seen enough.

He turned to Angus. "This is sick; I'm getting out . . . you coming?"

"I'm right behind you."

It seemed that Fanshawe was also becoming impatient, unlike the rest of the audience who, judging by the delirious shrieking and whooping, were settled in for the afternoon. He nudged Trinculo to indicate that they were leaving, but Trinculo, Monk, and Shakespeare were engrossed in the proceedings in the bear pit and elected to stay. Thus Jack and Angus left the greatest-ever genius of the English language to while away an enjoyable afternoon watching various animals maul one another to death.

They left the bearbaiting pit and continued west along the river. On the other side of the river they could see Saint Paul's cathedral silhouetted against the gray winter sky. Its spire was oddly stunted as a result of damage from a lightning strike years before. In the far distance were the abbey and palace of Westminster. Also across the river, but nearer to them, were the palaces of Whitehall, the Savoy, and other dwellings of the nobility. Their gardens extended all the way down to the river, and most had watergates for easy access to the riverboats.

"The Paris Gardens," Fanshawe announced airily as they entered an area of open park next to the river. "We will take a boat back across the river from here so I can find Walsingham and deliver Marlowe's letter, hopefully in time to protect the Queen."

They moved through the gardens and approached the pier where riverboats and wherries touted for business. A tall man approached them from the pier. Jack thought he looked a little out of place compared to the other rivermen. He had a dark tan, and his clothes appeared to be well-made, including a fine black cloak.

"Gentlemen, please take my boat—much warmer and more comfortable."

The boat had a large enclosed canopy on the back that protected its passengers from the elements.

"Why not?" Fanshawe said, and they boarded the boat and climbed into the canopy at the back. Outside they could hear two or three other people board the boat and a creak of oars as they glided away from the pier.

After a while the tall man entered the canopy. He was followed by a second man who also had dark skin and a powerful frame. He had one badly disfigured eye and a scar that stretched from his forehead across the side of his eye and down his cheek. There was something oddly familiar about the man. There was something else, of more concern. Both men were pointing heavy matchlock pistols at them.

The tall man spoke. "If you make any noise—you will die."

Into Thin Air

Their hands were tied behind their backs and hoods placed over their heads. Fanshawe began to sob.

The man repeated his threat. "I said no noise."

It was difficult to tell in which direction they were going, but after twenty minutes the rocking of the boat stopped. Jack felt a jab in his ribs and then a heavy hand guided him, still blindfolded, from the boat and onto some stone steps that rose up from the river. By peering down his nose, Jack could just make out the terrain and avoided stumbling.

"Where are you taking us?" Angus demanded.

Jack heard a dull thud, and Angus groaned.

"I said no talking."

Though they could not have been far from the city it was oddly quiet. After a few minutes they entered a building. Although he still had his hood on, Jack could tell that it must have been a reasonably large place because there was stone paving beneath his feet and a slight echo as they were marched inside. Maybe it was one of the large houses that they had seen from the south bank of the river. They stopped, and Jack could hear the men talking among themselves—in Spanish. He know then that their captors must be the same people whom they had barely escaped in Cambridge.

He heard a key turn in a lock and they were pushed forward again.

"Down," the man said.

Jack stepped down a staircase that smelled damp and musty. When they had been outside, daylight had filtered through his hood, but now everything was completely black. The rope around his wrists was beginning to rub. They reached the bottom of the staircase, and Jack felt himself being manhandled across a room and pushed up against a cold wall. Some kind of metal cuff was placed around his ankle and he heard the clanging of a heavy chain. Suddenly, the hood was ripped from his head. At first he did not understand what he was looking at, but then as the features of the room before him slowly came into focus, he felt an overwhelming sense of terror.

All three of them were manacled to a brick wall which formed one side of a large cellar. The only light came from candles, which flickered in the gloom. Directly in front of them was a rectangular wooden frame, slightly raised from the ground. The strange device had rollers inserted into the frame and two metal bars at each end. Attached to the bars were looped rope fasteners. There was a large lever attached to the top bar and this, in turn, linked to a system of chains and pulleys within the structure. With growing horror, Jack realized what the strange machine was—a torture rack. The limbs of the victim were tied to the bars with the rope fasteners. The handle and ratchet attached to the top roller were used to gradually increase the tension on the chains, which in turn strained the ropes, eventually causing the victim's joints to be dislocated, inducing excruciating pain. The machine before them was designed to tear its victim limb from limb.

Fanshawe howled uncontrollably. Without hesitation, the swarthy man with the scar slapped him with the back of his hand across his face.

"Shut up!" he said.

Fanshawe's howls degenerated into intermittent sobbing.

"Enough." The tall, well-dressed man stepped forward from the shadows.

He gestured to the rack. "You like our *potro*? Or if you wish, we have the *garrucha*." He pointed to a beam on the ceiling to which an elaborate pulley system was attached. On one of the wooden tables in the cellar there was an array of stone and metal blocks. The torture consisted of suspending the victim from the ceiling with weights tied to the ankles. Through the lifting and dropping of the weights, the victim's arms and legs suffered violent pulls and were sometimes dislocated. Fanshawe could not control himself and wailed again. The thug raised his hand, and this time it was enough to silence Fanshawe.

"Or maybe the *tortura del agua*?" Again the man gestured casually to a number of large flagons of water set out on the stone floor.

Despite his fear, Jack recognized the word "agua." He tried to remember what it meant. *Water. Waterboarding. He's talking about waterboarding.* He had heard the expression and knew it consisted of putting a cloth into the mouth of the victim and forcing them to ingest water so that they felt like they were drowning.

The tall man spoke good English. He was calm and polite, and his manner contrasted with the horror of the instruments before them. It somehow made the threat even worse.

"You may call me Señor Delgado." He nodded toward the two thugs who glowered back at them. "My friends here are Hegel and Plato. Now, so we are all clear, I do not wish to use any of our special equipment. But my friends here, I am afraid, need little encouragement. You understand, of course. So you will help us." He walked over to Fanshawe, standing next to Jack, and smiled at him. Then he reached down inside Fanshawe's doublet. Fanshawe squealed. Delgado pulled out the sealed document that Fanshawe had placed there for safekeeping.

"Finally, we have it." He broke the seal and opened the letter, holding it close to one of the candles. There was an eerie silence as he read.

"As we thought." He placed the letter back on the table. "You will tell us all you know about this letter—how you got it and what else you know of our plans."

"I don't know anything. I have not even read it," Fanshawe gibbered.

Without hesitation, the man clicked his fingers. Immediately, Plato and Hegel approached, unshackled Fanshawe, and dragged him over to the rack. He kicked and screamed as they lowered him onto the evil device. They were much too strong for him, and in a second they had tied his legs to the lower bar and his arms to the upper bar. Plato put both his hands onto the long lever and looked across at his boss. He grinned as he eagerly awaited the signal to continue.

"Wait!" Jack shouted. Delgado wheeled around. "We were given the letter in Cambridge . . ."

"Don't lie," Delgado spat in frustration. "Marlowe works for us and he is safe now—he told us what happened. You were going to kill him unless he told you about the plot. You forced him to write the letter. We arrived before you could finish your work. You escaped us in Cambridge, but now we have you. You work for Walsingham and you know Walsingham's other spies. We want their names."

Angus shouted out furiously, "That's ridiculous—we don't know anything! Fanshawe was asked by Marlowe to deliver this letter for money. That's all we know."

Anger flashed across Delgado's face. "You lie!" He clicked his fingers and Plato pulled the lever. There was a creaking of rope and wood as the rack strained. Fanshawe screamed. It was not a human scream.

"Your friend will die there if I do not have the truth."

"Marlowe's tricked you!" Jack shouted in desperation.

"Before we continue, we search you for more papers."

The man pointed to Hegel, who loped over to Angus and pawed at his clothes.

He reached into Angus's doublet, searching for anything that might be valuable or useful. He patted the breast pocket of Angus's vest and felt a lump. He looked over at Delgado with a curious leer and then slowly removed the slim object from the pocket. It was his time phone.

Hegel held it out to Delgado with a look of confusion. Delgado approached.

"What is that?" he demanded.

Angus looked at Jack with an expression of extreme agitation. Their situation was desperate. Jack fought his panic and fear, struggling to think clearly, to think of a way, any way, they could believably explain the time phones. Suddenly, out of nowhere, he had an idea. It was a long shot, but . . .

"It's a kind of lucky charm. We have them, er, from where we come from," Jack said.

"Is it valuable?"

"Not really, but you can open it."

"Show me."

"You'll have to untie me."

Delgado nodded at Hegel to release Jack's hands, though his feet remained firmly chained to the wall. Jack rubbed his wrists, which were already raw from chafing on the rope.

"It is a wondrous thing," Hegel said in awe. "Plato, come look at this!"

Plato left Fanshawe still roped to the rack and ambled over to where his friends toyed with the time phone.

"It is made of a strange smooth material—like shell."

"Carbon-fiber compound, actually," Jack said, under his breath.

"And you say it opens?"

"Yes, you slide that on the side . . . and . . . there."

The VIGIL time phone slid open, and the three men's faces lit up with wonder as the intricate display and controls were revealed.

"Like a jewel. Do you have others?"

Before Jack could say anything, Plato was searching him roughly and quickly located Jack's time phone and the two others that they had taken from Whitsun and Gift.

"Four!" Hegel exclaimed.

The Spaniards now had all the time phones. Jack had won them a temporary reprieve, but then he noticed something else, something he had been hoping for but still couldn't believe. From inside the first time phone, the yellow bar winked brightly at them. There was a time signal.

"It produces a shimmering light . . ." Delgado said.

"It must be magic," Plato whispered in wonder.

Jack knew what he needed to do next, and he knew he was taking a huge risk. But it was their only option.

"If you like I can show you something else it does. But you need to stand there, all together, and touch it."

The three other time phones were discarded on a nearby table while the men gingerly placed their fingers on Angus's time phone. "Now it does a special trick. . . . You see that little button there."

"This one?" Delgado asked, pointing at one of the small control pads.

"Yes, that one. You have to press it quite hard."

"What will it do?"

"Nothing really. Just a little, trick . . . er, a trick of the light."

Delgado pressed the button, and Jack closed his eyes and leaned away.

The air around the three men shimmered. Suddenly the gloomy cellar exploded in incandescent white light. When Jack reopened his eyes, the three Spaniards had vanished into thin air.

Jack turned to Angus. "Now, *that* is magic."

An Old Friend

Get me out of this!" Angus said.

Jack was still manacled to the wall, but his hands were free. He just managed to reach over to Angus beside him and loosen the rope around his wrists sufficiently for Angus to twist them free.

"What about these stupid chains?"

"You've got me there." The heavy iron manacles still encased their ankles, and each was chained to the wall.

"There should be a key somewhere . . ."

"Unless it was in the pocket of our nice Spanish friend and zapped into hyperspace. You do realize what you've done?"

Jack exhaled. "Sorry, it was all I could think of at the time."

Angus's lip curled up in a half smile. "Actually, pretty cool. Hilarious, in fact. What will happen to them?"

"No idea. Depends on the space-time fix in the time phone. Guess it was still set from when we left, so maybe they will go straight back to the Taurus, and our VIGIL friends back home will have a little surprise when they come face-to-face with the Spanish Inquisition."

"With any luck they've been vaporized instead. Those guys were something else. I'd love to see their faces if the Taurus has zapped them onto the top of the Forth Road Bridge . . . or the Statue of Liberty or something by mistake."

"We've got other things to worry about. We have a time signal so all the time phones should be activated. Which means we could time travel out of here, except for the fact that we're still tied to these stupid chains and the other time phones are over there."

In the excitement, they had forgotten all about Fanshawe, who was still attached to the rack in the middle of the room. In contrast to a few minutes prior, he was completely silent. He stared dully from his elevated position on the rack at the spot where the three Spaniards had just . . . disappeared. His jaw hung loosely from a gaping mouth.

"Are you OK, Harry?"

It was as if Fanshawe had not even heard the words. He just kept staring into space.

Jack tried again, louder. "Harry, you OK? Can you free yourself and get us out of these chains?"

Fanshawe blinked. He whispered, "It is a miracle. We are saved. . . ."

"Yeah. Something like that," Angus said.

"But . . . how . . ." Poor old Fanshawe had endured complete sensory overload in the last hour. He had been kidnapped, tortured, and now he had seen three grown men vanish into thin air.

Jack sighed in frustration. "Harry, we need you to try and work yourself free of that thing and unchain us."

It was no use. Even if Fanshawe had been in the appropriate mental state, which he wasn't, he was firmly tied up.

"What now?" Angus said.

"If VIGIL is doing their job properly, they should have a space-time fix on this location and time through the time phones."

"But the Revisionists' time phones are also activated, so they also will know where we are."

"Assuming Whitsun and Gift have escaped and reconnected with Pendelshape and any other Revisionists and told them that we have their phones."

"So we just have to wait and see who gets here first?" Angus pulled on the chain again in frustration. But it was hopeless. They had gotten rid of the Spaniards, but they were still stuck.

"What's that?" Jack said suddenly.

"Footsteps? Upstairs in the house? Someone's here already."

"But is it VIGIL or the Revisionists?"

"Or someone else?"

There was an almighty crash as the cellar door was forced open and splinters of wood rained down the stone stairs. Next, they heard someone gingerly making their way down the steps into the cellar.

Angus and Jack craned their heads to try and make out the figure, but from their position chained to the wall, their view was impaired. Then a powerful beam of light shone toward them.

Jack whispered to Angus, "A flashlight?"

Initially, they were unable to recognize the figure silhouetted behind the bright light.

"Good evening, gentlemen. It looks like I got here just in time."

The voice was unmistakable. Dr. Pendelshape.

Pendelshape scanned the room quickly to make sure there was no one else there. He then turned his attention to Jack and Angus.

"We don't have much time. We need to get you out of those chains."

"We don't know where the key is."

Pendelshape searched the wooden tabletops. The first things he spotted were the remaining three time phones laid out on one of the tables.

"At least we have those back," he said. "And an extra one . . . a VIGIL time phone." He smiled. "Now that is going to come in handy." He opened each of them in turn and powered them down. "Disconnected—we don't want anyone else to know where we are for now, do we?"

He quickly looked through the boys' backpacks that had been left on the floor. He spotted the two pistols belonging to Whitsun and Gift.

"And I think you're still a bit young to be carrying firearms."

Next, he discovered the letter from Marlowe, now opened, which Delgado had taken from Fanshawe. Pendelshape read it quickly. "As we thought—this confirms what we already know." He put the letter back on the table and pulled out a pocketknife-type gadget.

"Let's try this." He flicked out a couple of different key-shaped arms and began to work on jimmying the locks. Soon Jack and Angus were free.

"I have a carriage waiting outside that can take us to safety. If we stay here we run a high risk of being found." He paused and looked over at Fanshawe. "I'm afraid there is one final piece of business."

Pendelshape opened his doublet. Beneath it, he wore a tight fitting vest—similar to those worn by the boys. It had a number of pockets, and Jack noticed that one was shaped like a holster. Pendelshape pulled out a pistol and matter-of-factly strode over to where Fanshawe lay and pointed the gun at his head. The action closely mimicked that of Whitsun and Gift outside Cambridge only a few days before.

"No!" Jack screamed.

Pendelshape swiveled around, a bemused expression on his face. "No?"

"You can't just *kill* him!"

"He's seen too much. He knows too much about the plot. He may ruin all of our plans."

Jack was outraged that Pendelshape, just like Whitsun and Gift, could contemplate such a barbaric act—and do it so casually.

"But, but . . . he knows nothing. The poor guy has simply been a messenger. He doesn't know who you are—or even who we really are, for that matter. He is utterly harmless."

Fanshawe, still attached to the rack, was slowly regaining his senses. Fanshawe begged, "I do not know anything . . . *please* . . ."

Pendelshape thought for a moment and shrugged. "So be it, then; I will release you. You have young Jack here to thank. But you must leave this house. If you return or speak of any of these events, you will risk your life. Do you understand?"

The decision not to murder Fanshawe was made as easily as the decision seconds before to kill him. Jack was staggered by Pendelshape's casual disregard for human life. Fanshawe looked at Pendelshape and then back at Jack. Jack nodded. Fanshawe sobbed with relief. Jack had saved his life twice in one day.

They emerged from the cellar into a large kitchen at the back of the house. It was now nighttime, and there was only the light from Pendelshape's flashlight and a few candles that had been left to burn down. Pendelshape led them to the front door of the house and out into a clear, cold night. A small carriage waited with a driver a little farther down the road.

Pendelshape pointed out Fanshawe's route. "That way—it will take you to Ludgate eventually. And remember what I told you," he added menacingly.

"Yes, sir. Thank you, sir," Fanshawe said. Fanshawe shook Angus's hand and then glanced toward Pendelshape and the carriage before putting both his hands over Jack's hands and looking him in the eye. "Thank you, Jack, for all you have done for me." Then he whispered, "I will repay you."

Pendelshape was getting impatient, and he boomed out at Fanshawe, "Go!"

Fanshawe scurried off into the night.

Pendelshape turned to the carriage driver and whispered some instructions.

"You two in there. No funny business—we have a lot of catching up to do."

Jack and Angus had little choice.

They all climbed into the carriage, and it rumbled off. Soon Jack and then Angus, drained by a traumatic day, fell asleep.

The carriage picked its way up the bumpy road and away from the riverside mansions. An hour after it had melted into the night, two furtive figures appeared at the door of the house that the group had left not long before. After an initial check outside, the two men proceeded to break into the house and search it. They found it empty except for the sinister torture equipment secreted in its cellar. If Jack and Angus had left the house only a little later, they would have finally met up with Tony and Gordon, their comrades from VIGIL.

The Beautiful Game

Where are we?" Jack asked. He peered through a small window at a muddy farmyard. The fields beyond had been dusted white from a light flurry of snow.

"Wembley Stadium," Pendelshape said matter-of-factly as he busied himself at a small woodstove. He was cooking eggs and bacon, and he had already managed to produce a pot of very acceptable coffee somehow. He seemed to be completely at home. "Not literally, of course. It's where Wembley Stadium will be in the future. This area is where the locker rooms will be, and you're probably sitting exactly where the England team would be getting changed." He craned his head to view the frozen farmland that stretched into the distance. "As you can see, it's a pretty far cry from the view out there today." He served the eggs and bacon on three dishes and placed them on the table. Jack was ravenous, and the food smelled incredibly good.

Pendelshape had based himself in a farmer's cottage. He had negotiated a generous rent in return for complete privacy for the duration of his stay. The cottage was on two floors—a higgledy-piggledy oak-frame construction. It was well-appointed, and when the fire got going, the house warmed up quickly. In any case, when they had arrived in the carriage the night before, Jack had been so exhausted that he was asleep as soon he had gotten into bed.

Pendelshape ate slowly and from time to time would eye Jack and Angus thoughtfully. He had not really changed. Maybe he had shed some weight from his portly frame, but the crow's feet around his deep-set eyes and the cropped gray hair were still the same. The last time Jack had seen Pendelshape was in a First World War trench six months ago. That was when he had showed Jack and Angus the true horrors of war in a final attempt to get them to desert VIGIL and to join Jack's father and himself. Jack and Angus saw the horrors of war all right—Pendelshape's badly conceived escapade nearly got them killed. It was the final straw for Jack, and it was the moment that finally convinced him that meddling in history was too dangerous, however well-planned and well-meaning. It was also the moment when he realized that Pendelshape had a screw loose. Jack had seen him turn from being his affable but eccentric history teacher into a fanatic who would stop at nothing to get his own way.

"So, gentlemen, it would appear that we have some decisions to make." Pendelshape spoke calmly, but Jack could feel the menace in his voice. "Or to be more precise, you have some decisions to make. But first of all, I should perhaps explain what you have embroiled yourselves in. I have to say that you have been extremely lucky to escape with your lives."

"I think we know that," Angus said through a mouthful of bacon.

Pendelshape ignored him. "First things first. I am sure you will be pleased to hear that my colleagues, Mr. Whitsun and Mr. Gift, have recovered. I understand from them that you two had nothing to do with their injuries . . . which I am glad to hear about. They have learned a valuable lesson."

"Where are they?" Jack asked.

"They managed to make it to our rendezvous point . . . somewhat worse for wear, and they have now been deployed elsewhere, ready for the next stage of our plan. We will meet them later."

"What were they doing in Cambridge—and how did they know we were there?"

"The people who chased you were Spanish spies that Marlowe works for. But what they don't know is that he also works for Walsingham—Queen Elizabeth's spymaster. Marlowe is a double agent. The letter contains details of a plot against the English state."

"What kind of plot?"

"As you know, Jack, this is a dangerous period in history. Philip II of Spain has finally lost his patience with England. English ships have continued to steal from Spanish ships. Under Elizabeth, England is a Protestant country—Catholics are tolerated; however, there is much tension between them. The execution of Mary, Queen of Scots a few days ago was the final straw. Mary was implicated in a plot to overthrow Elizabeth, and for this, she was executed. Killing a fellow monarch is a grave act. Philip is mobilizing a mighty navy— the Armada—to capture the English throne and finally get rid of Elizabeth."

"But I thought the Armada gets defeated," Angus said.

"It does. The whole thing is badly conceived, badly planned, and badly executed. In addition, the Spanish do not account for the English superiority in ship design, gunnery, and tactics. And finally, of course, there is the weather—the storms which finally scatter Philip's great ships off the coasts of Scotland and Ireland. Half of the Armada's one hundred and thirty ships will be lost or irreparably damaged. England will lose no ships. The loss of Spanish crew and soldiers will be severe. Two-thirds of the Armada's thirty thousand men will die— and for every one killed in battle, another seven will perish from execution, drowning, disease, starvation, or thirst."

Pendelshape had a glint in his eye as spoke. It was as if Jack was back in his history class.

"The Armada will be a tragedy. And from that point on, the balance of power in the world will gradually tip in England's favor. The defeat of the Armada is a turning point."

"But why does this concern you? You're not just on a visit, are you?"

"No, Jack, as I'm quite sure you are aware." He refilled his cup. "Let me show you something."

Pendelshape got to his feet and walked over to a case on the other side of the kitchen. He opened it up and took out a slim laptop and placed it on the table in front of them. The device looked completely out of place in the old kitchen.

"Nice computer, sir." Angus had not quite gotten out of the habit of calling Pendelshape sir.

"Indeed. But you won't find this one on the market at home. We've had to make a number of modifications to run our simulation software." He tapped the keyboard. "Now, this should do it. Yes, you can take a look if you like."

Pendelshape swiveled the screen around to allow Jack and Angus a better view. It showed a picture of the Earth. In one corner there were the words, *Timeline Simulator,* and in the other the date and time. There were a number of complicated toolbars at the bottom left of the screen.

"So this is a political representation of the world as it is now in February, 1587. You can see England and Scotland—two different kingdoms, of course—France, and the Italian city-states. And there is Spain shaded in yellow. You can already see Spain has taken over much of what's now called the New World—Central and South America, and also in other places like the Netherlands. In fact, it is the Duke of Parma's army in the Netherlands that Philip II plans to transport to England using the Armada to defeat the English. You can see from the coloring on the map that Spain is a major power, although what you don't see is the vast wealth of Spain from the stream of gold and especially silver from the New World. Anyway, look what happens if I run the simulation forward. I'll do the baseline simulation first—this shows what happens if you don't make any interventions in history as it currently stands."

Pendelshape touched the screen, and the year counter on the right started to count forward the months and the years.

Angus was impressed. "Cool."

Jack rolled his eyes.

As the years counted forward the colors on the map grew and shrank in line with the political influence of the various countries of the world. The yellow of Spain began to shrink. The small red blob that denoted England slowly started to grow. First, it extended to Scotland and then to North America. As the year counter ticked its way through the nineteenth century, the red shading grew across all parts of the world like some sort of infectious disease—India, Australia, Africa—the British Empire. At the same time, the development of the other European nations and their power across the world was shown—the blue of France and the black of a unified Germany.

The counter then moved on through the twentieth century to show the rise of the Soviet Union and the United States and the decline of the old European countries.

"It's like a game," Angus said.

Jack was a little less impressed. "Looks nice—but what does it mean?"

"Jack, this is the Timeline Simulator—or at least the results of it—the full thing is too resource-intensive even for this mighty machine. This software is the key to it all. . . ."

"Key to what?"

Pendelshape sighed. "Let me explain. The members of VIGIL refuse to accept that the Taurus can be used as a tool for good."

"Yes. And they have a point. We saw what could happen when we went back to the First World War," Jack said.

"You nearly got us all killed, sir," Angus said bluntly.

"I admit, at that time, we thought we had it right—but we were still not quite there. VIGIL's concern is that by intervening in the past you can trigger changes, however well-intentioned, that may have unforeseen consequences in the future."

"Yes, and it can be extremely dangerous. Intervening can backfire and lead to even worse things happening," Jack said.

"And VIGIL is right up to a point. But this"—Pendelshape tapped the laptop with a chubby index finger—"this little thing changes everything. We have developed causal models of history to such a degree that we can show precisely the impact that changes we make in the past will have on the future. We can also evaluate the different scenarios that arise from this. If necessary we can make subsequent interventions in time to optimize the results. These interventions may also be used to ensure that we can keep the Revisionist team untouched." He smiled knowingly. "Obviously there are some things in the present that we want to remain untouched."

Angus finally finished his breakfast. "So what?"

"So what, Angus," Pendelshape continued, a note of frustration in his voice, "so what is that we can make measurements of our scenarios. We can evaluate changes we make in terms of their impact on economic wealth, political stability, health, and a whole range of other things, including—believe it or not—an index of human happiness."

This was too much even for Angus. "You've got to be kidding me, sir. You're saying that you can use that computer to say, for instance, what would happen to the world if you assassinated Hitler, and measure how happy everyone would be as a result."

"Indeed. It sounds strange, I know, but every scenario has upsides and downsides, winners and losers. What we are seeking to do is to find the best overall scenario that optimizes human well-being in the long term—and for that matter the well-being of the planet. And, yes, we can't really do the comparison unless we can measure the scenarios. Happiness is one of those measures. All the measures together are called the Utility Index—the UI."

"So you are saying that you have managed to develop the software to a point where you can really run sort of 'what-ifs' and measure the impact."

"Yes, Jack, exactly."

Jack lowered his voice. "But Dad didn't agree with your plans, did he?"

Pendelshape sighed. "We had a disagreement with your father. We were keen to use our Taurus with the new Timeline Simulator, but your father refused until he was sure that you were safely removed from VIGIL's control. Their control over you and your father's fear of what they might do to you, should we act, was the main thing that prevented us from doing anything with the new system. But he also wanted you to join us—he has always wanted you to follow in his footsteps. We became impatient, the arguments became more heated, and eventually . . ."

"Eventually what?"

"The team and I decided to remove him as leader of the Revisionists. He left of his own accord. However, we knew he might do something unpredictable. We knew that there was a risk that he would contact VIGIL and tell them of our plans to prevent them from thinking he was still in charge and that this was all his idea. He was worried about you . . . and your mother. Your presence here confirms that he did indeed warn VIGIL—although why on earth VIGIL decided to send you and Angus back on a mission as important as this, I have no idea."

Angus said sheepishly, "It hasn't exactly gone according to plan."

"But you still haven't explained what intervention you plan to make," Jack said.

Pendelshape gazed out the window, which was starting to mist up from the warmth in the room. He seemed to be weighing something in his mind—something important. "I suppose it makes no difference now," he said, turning back to the screen. "Let me show you."

He punched the keyboard again and leaned back. "Here. You can see."

The year counter was reset to 1587, and again the days, months, and years ticked forward. This time, something strange happened on the map. The yellow denoting the extent of Spain's geographical and political power did not decline as before. Instead, first England turned yellow, and then gradually the whole of South America, North America, and Western Europe. As the years ticked through the nineteenth century some other colors—blue, black, red—did appear on the screen, but they failed to expand as they had before. They seemed to be quickly snuffed out by the yellow shading, which continued its onward march until, as the year approached 1894, it engulfed almost the entire world.

Jack stared in wonder at the screen. "Spain rules the entire world? Is that what that means?"

"Not quite. Spain conquers England, of course, and in time that gives rise to what becomes an Anglo-Spanish hegemony—the power base eventually moves to the Americas and that becomes a basis for global domination. What we see here starts with Spain—but over time it morphs into something different and new."

"And that's a good thing?"

"You miss the point. It's a *better* thing. Very high UI—in the long term."

"But isn't that against, I don't know, rules—things like, people should be free to choose who governs them, democracy, and all that stuff?"

"There is a place for democracy, in time, and a democratic global state does emerge from this—eventually. The point is that there are no countries, as such—all artificial boundaries are destroyed as the super-state develops. At points, as in any historical process, there is brutality, and special interests have to be crushed. But you can only achieve stability through strong leadership and control. Because in the long term what emerges is much better—certainly better than having hundreds of different countries that can't agree on anything and keep having wars."

As Jack stared at the picture of the world in front of him, entirely shaded in yellow, it dawned on him that the ambition of the Revisionists and of Pendelshape was utterly astonishing. They planned to use the Taurus to rip apart the fabric of history and start again. It was mind-blowing. Jack could see that this ability to play God would be hugely seductive—particularly for someone like Pendelshape.

"How will you do it?"

"The first steps are very simple. First Spain must defeat England. The new nation that forms from this must then be guided at points through the subsequent centuries—with an occasional hand on the tiller from us. The scenario is also modeled to ensure that the Revisionist team and our Taurus are protected. Off-limits, if you will."

"How is England defeated?" Angus asked.

"Ideally, we need to make two interventions. First, Queen Elizabeth must die. This will result in a power vacuum and internal strife in England—civil war, actually. This first step is desirable, but not completely essential. Secondly, and more importantly, we need the Armada to succeed. A key point is the battle of Gravelines, which was a key English victory during the Armada. If that can be reversed, then the Armada will succeed, laying the way for a successful Spanish invasion. With a successful Spanish invasion, order will be restored and we start the next stage of our work."

"So this plot that we stumbled across with Marlowe . . . I guess that has something to do with part one of your plan—the death of Elizabeth."

"Indeed. We researched the period extensively to identify a

suitable opportunity. We considered the Babington Plot and using Mary, Queen of Scots, but dismissed the idea. Our plan is to avoid an obvious successor to maximize a period of internal strife in England before the arrival of the Spanish. Of course, this period is rife with espionage. Your Spanish friends from yesterday have a well-developed plan, and Whitsun, Gift, and I are here to make sure it goes smoothly. When Whitsun and Gift discovered that you were in Cambridge, they knew they had to act quickly to remove you so you couldn't do anything to alter their plans."

"Alter their plans?"

"Yes. But Whitsun and Gift failed, and now, of course, your actions in the torture chamber have changed everything. The Spanish assassination cell will shortly discover that three of their colleagues have mysteriously disappeared, and they will very likely abandon the plot."

Jack tried to follow Pendelshape's logic. "So, now that this has all happened, your next step must be to infiltrate the assassination cell to make sure that the plot still goes ahead. Right?"

"Correct. With Elizabeth dead, stage one is complete."

"How do you, er . . . they plan to kill her?"

Pendelshape refilled the boys' mugs. "That, my dear boy, would be a little too much information. But it is all set out in the letter that Marlowe gave you. That is why it was important to intercept the letter and prevent it from getting to Walsingham. Without it, and with Marlowe safely in the hands of the Spanish, Walsingham and the crown are none the wiser." Pendelshape patted his sides absentmindedly. "In fact, where did I put the letter?" Jack and Angus looked at each other. "No matter—I will find it in a minute. . . . Anyway—we know all details of the Spanish plot, and it will not take much to get it back on track. Everything is in position."

Jack's head was spinning as he tried to assimilate what Pendelshape had said. There was one question that their old teacher had not answered.

"Why are you telling us all this?"

Pendelshape paused before he spoke. "We need to make some decisions. Or to be more precise—*you* do."

Jack's brow furrowed.

"It's your choice, really. You can come with me and join the Revisionists—just like we offered you before. Your father is right— just like VIGIL, we must also seek to train the next generation of Revisionists. The irony of this great power we have, this power to change history, is that we are still mortal. I will not be here forever. We need to recruit and train new followers to continue our work. They will ensure that the course of history continues to be maintained for the benefit of the human race. Who better than yourselves to start this process? With you on our side, your father, with his great intellectual gifts, will rejoin us, and there will be nothing to stop us. VIGIL will be destroyed and we will change the world and then keep it changed— for good. This is the opportunity before you." His eyes glinted. "To spell it out—I am offering you one final chance."

"And if we don't join you?"

Pendelshape quietly reached into his holster and pulled out the pistol they had seen him wield in the cellar. He pointed it across the table at them. "If you choose not to, I'm afraid you leave me with no option—I do not have the same family concerns as your father. If you continue to side with VIGIL and meddle in our plans, you must be removed. If and when I see your father again, I will explain, with great sorrow of course, that you were—what's the expression? *Collateral damage.*"

He cocked the gun.

"I need your decision, gentlemen."

Appointment at the Palace

Pendelshape held the gun steadily, two feet from Jack's face. Jack's heart raced. He had already witnessed the casual attitude that Pendelshape had toward human life. Jack had no doubt that Pendelshape would carry out his threat. The irony was, of course, that Pendelshape was giving them exactly the opportunity that Inchquin had hoped for when VIGIL had sent them back. Their mission was to gain Pendelshape's confidence and infiltrate the Revisionists. On the spur of the moment at VIGIL HQ it had seemed like a good idea; but now, faced with the reality, it was frightening and confusing. Without contact with Tony and Gordon, they had no support, no backup, and no way of communicating with VIGIL. But with Pendelshape's pistol hanging menacingly in the air in front of them, it was also their only option.

From outside the small kitchen window Jack heard a strange noise. It was a sort of muffled jangling. Suddenly an object appeared outside the window. The object arced slowly from the left side of the window across to the right. As the object moved, it bobbed up and down. The window was fogged up, so it was difficult to make out what it actually was. But it was colorful. In fact, it had yellow and red stripes. As far as Jack could discern, for some inexplicable reason, a large jester's hat seemed to be flying backward and forward outside their window with no visible means of support. Pendelshape was understandably distracted by the strange apparition. He rubbed the misted window to get a better look.

"What on earth . . . ?"

Suddenly, the small wooden door on the opposite side of the kitchen flew open. Incredibly, Harry Fanshawe stood in the doorway brandishing a full-length musket—he looked almost as scared as Jack and Angus. For a moment the musket wobbled uneasily in his hands. Pendelshape swiveled away from the window and jumped to his feet, leveling his pistol at Fanshawe. Fanshawe panicked, shut his eyes, and pulled the trigger of his mighty blunderbuss. The flintlock slammed down into the breach and there was an odd delay before the powder inside ignited. When it did, it was as if the whole house had been detonated. The musket recoiled so hard it lifted Fanshawe off his feet and threw him a full six feet back through the kitchen door. Pendelshape screamed as the crude lead shot from the musket embedded itself in his thigh. He immediately fell to the ground, clutching his leg with one hand. Somehow he had the presence of mind to retain his grip on the pistol and squeeze the trigger. The bullet flew into the ceiling, and a large dollop of plaster and wood rained on the room.

Before Pendelshape could fire again, Angus heaved the wooden kitchen table on its side and, using it as a shield, he and Jack retreated from the kitchen. Pendelshape squirmed on the floor, but with the boys protected by the screen of wood, he was unable to get a clear shot. He roared in frustration and fired off a volley of shots. The table in Angus's hands jarred violently as each bullet hit; the wood splintered but was not holed. They reached the door and Angus dropped the table, leaving it as a horizontal barrier across the threshold. They pulled Fanshawe back to his feet and sprinted out of the cottage and into the yard, leaving Pendelshape trapped but still armed inside.

Outside, Trinculo and Monk had four horses ready. Trinculo put away his jester's hat, which, with the use of a large stick poked inside, had been the source of Pendelshape's distraction. Angus pulled Jack up to ride behind him.

"Let's go!" Fanshawe shouted, and galloped off.

But Angus waited. "Are we just going to leave him there?"

"What choice do we have? He's well-equipped—he's not going to die."

"That's what I mean, Jack. We could end it all right here."

"He's armed—in case you didn't notice."

"We could burn the cottage down or something."

Jack punched Angus in the back. "You're not serious! He might be mad—and he might be OK with going around killing people randomly, but remember what I said before—we're not—right?"

"Yeah, right. Sorry. So what, then? Try and take him prisoner or something? Remember our mission."

Their conversation was cut short. The front door of the cottage flew open and Pendelshape staggered toward them, zombie-like, brandishing his pistol and firing wildly.

"OK, screw the mission." Angus jabbed his heels into the horse and they shot off down the farm path after Fanshawe, Monk, and Trinculo.

It took them two hours to travel back into London. They eventually located a small pub in one of the maze of roads off Eastcheap. As usual, the city was mobbed, and even assuming that Pendelshape recovered from the wound Fanshawe had inflicted, he would never find them there.

"So why did you come back, Harry?" Jack asked as they huddled around a small table at the back of the inn.

"It's simple, Jack; you saved my life, and I could tell that man was trouble. I decided to follow you."

"To the farm?"

"Yes. Late last night I returned to find help, and Trinculo and Monk agreed to come with me this morning. We got the musket from the Rose Theater. It is used on stage sometimes. We brought it just in case. But then it all happened so quickly." There was a pause as Fanshawe looked at Jack with a serious expression. "What's going on, Jack? Who are all these people—the Spaniards, those men in Cambridge, the man in the farmhouse? And, and . . . what did you do to those men in the torture cellar?"

Fanshawe, Trinculo, and Monk stared at them. There was silence as Jack searched for inspiration. "We're not sure either, Harry, but we seem to have all gotten ourselves caught up in something that we shouldn't have. I think it all started when we met Marlowe. The letter from Marlowe says that there is a Spanish plot against England.

Marlowe is a double agent—he works for the Spanish but also for Walsingham. He betrayed us to save his own skin. They tracked us down to London to stop us from giving the letter to Walsingham and uncovering the plot."

Fanshawe looked confused. "But what about—what did you call him—Pendelwright?"

"Pendelshape. He's one of the plotters—a fanatical Catholic." Jack had to lie. "He removed us from the house because it was too dangerous there once the others had gone, but he wanted to try to get more information out of us."

"And that . . ." Fanshawe's eyes opened in wonder. "Your magic orb—how did it make them disappear?"

Jack's imagination was working overtime. "It's a weapon, Harry. Italian—they're always coming up with strange stuff. We got to know a couple of older students from Genoa . . . when we were at Cambridge. They, er, sold one to us . . . You know what it's like these days—you need to be able to defend yourself." It was a terrible lie—but it was the best Jack could come up with. Anyway, the truth was even more unbelievable.

Fanshawe nodded and took a sip of beer. "Well, that's true. But they just *disappeared*. . . ." He stared unblinkingly into space as he recalled the moment.

Jack shrugged. "Sorry, Harry, I can't really explain it—there are more things in heaven and earth and all that . . ."

"So, shouldn't we warn Walsingham?" Trinculo said.

Jack shrugged. "Perhaps we should—but what would we say? Pendelshape took the letter from Marlowe and we don't really know anything about the plot, if you think about it—who or what it involves," Jack said. "Maybe we've already done enough through our actions to scare off the plotters. And I think there are plots and counterplots going on all the time—we might just find we draw more attention to ourselves."

Fanshawe took a long draught of ale and wiped his beard. Suddenly his demeanor changed, and he smiled.

"Well, at least we have some good news. We nearly forgot to tell you!" He nudged Trinculo. "My fine friend Trinculo has been busy. He has news which will make us all feel better." Fanshawe poked Trinculo in the ribs. "Go on, tell them."

"Yes, good news indeed. When you left the bearbaiting yesterday, Shakespeare, Monk, and I went back to the Rose to see if we could raise Henslowe. We found him!"

Fanshawe interrupted. "But not only that—tell them, Trinculo!"

"I'm trying to . . ."

"It would seem that Henslowe has a problem," Fanshawe continued enthusiastically.

Trinculo was getting annoyed by Fanshawe's interruptions. "He has a number of men down."

Fanshawe could contain himself no longer. "Yes! Three of his actors are ill. Very ill. Isn't that marvelous! They want us to replace them—well, at least temporarily. With any luck they won't recover. But more than that . . ."

"It gets better?"

"Much better. Henslowe is in a panic because in only two days' time his players will be performing at Hampton Court Palace." Fanshawe was beaming from ear to ear. "It is most excellently providential."

"Hampton Court Palace—who is he performing for?" Jack asked.

"The Queen herself, of course," Fanshawe replied.

Making an
Entrance

No! No! No!" For about the fifth time that morning, Thomas Kyd stormed onto the stage and advanced toward the troupe of actors rehearsing at the Rose. Kyd was proving to be demanding, irascible, and fussy. Perhaps it was fair enough. In two days' time they would perform his play in front of the Queen, her senior ministers, and a good section of the court at Hampton Court Palace. It would be the most important day of Kyd's life, and the lives of the Henslowe Players. Nevertheless, everyone had just about had enough, including the pompous Edward Alleyn, who, being the most famous actor of the day, was not used to being bossed around.

Jack and Angus sat at the rear of the stage under the wooden balcony. The inside of the Rose was like a smaller version of the bearbaiting pit, but in place of a large open arena the theater housed a wooden stage, raised about three feet off the ground, which projected out into the middle of the standing area. The stage and standing area were ringed by two levels of wooden galleries. The galleries were roofed, and the stage itself was given some protection by a raised balcony and large awning at the rear. Apart from this, the theater was open to the elements. There was garbage strewn everywhere, and the whole place smelled pretty bad.

Fanshawe and Trinculo had hit the jackpot when they had won parts for themselves in this prestigious play. Their timing could not have been better—Shakespeare, of course, knew Henslowe, who had built the theater. It also helped that the ambitious Shakespeare was well-acquainted with the famous actor Edward Alleyn and the playwright, Thomas Kyd. Despite these contacts, Fanshawe and Trinculo would not have stood a chance, if three of Henslowe's actors had not been taken ill and Henslowe and Kyd had not been desperate. The stakes could not have been higher. The date at Hampton Court in front of the Queen would be the inaugural performance of his masterpiece—*The Spanish Tragedy*.

There had only been one problem—and for this reason Angus had not stopped smiling since they had been allotted their parts. There was no role for Angus or Monk, but it did not matter because an extra pair of hands backstage was welcome. Jack was another matter altogether. The trouble was that the actor Jack was replacing had been a boy, perhaps a little younger than Jack, and the roles of women were always played by boys or men. The role that the boy had been playing was Isabella, the wife of Don Hieronimo. And so, Jack sat next to Angus wearing a dress.

"Shut up," Jack said for the umpteenth time that morning. "I have to learn these words. By tomorrow."

Angus laughed. "The things we do for VIGIL, eh? Don't worry, I think you look really nice."

Jack ignored him.

After a while, Angus lost interest in baiting Jack and pointed over at Kyd, who was still remonstrating with Alleyn. "They're still at it."

Jack glanced up from the script. "Well, they better get it sorted out—we haven't got much more time."

Jack and Angus sat in silence. Since their escape from Pendelshape, both of them had been particularly watchful. For about the tenth time, Angus said, "No time phones, no contact with VIGIL, so we just wait?"

"Yes. At least we're safe."

"You think?"

"Safe as anywhere."

"Well, I hope you're right." He nudged Jack. "Oh, here we go, looks like you're on. . . . Don't trip over your dress."

Jack got to his feet. "You're hilarious."

The rehearsal finally finished and the Henslowe Players prepared for their departure to Hampton Court Palace early the following morning. Hampton Court was upstream, so the decision had been made to transport them up the Thames by two boats. However, as they discovered the next morning, the two tilt boats that had been hired for the purpose were really too small to accommodate the entire cast of *The Spanish Tragedy,* their costumes, props, and various others—let alone the overgrown egos of Henslowe, Alleyn, and Kyd. Nevertheless, constrained by the limited budget set by Henslowe, who kept a beady eye on all costs, the two boats were going to have to do. Fortunately, the weather remained fine and the river was as smooth as a billiard table. Everyone was extremely glad to leave the rehearsals at the Rose and the endless differences of artistic opinion between Kyd and Alleyn.

There was lively chatter as everyone boarded the boats, which rapidly became overburdened. The river journey would take them slowly upriver, past Whitehall and then eventually to Richmond and Kingston. Just beyond Kingston, they would disembark and lodge at the magnificent Hampton Court Palace, where the Queen and her entourage were in temporary residence. The following afternoon they would stage the inaugural performance of *The Spanish Tragedy.* With luck, this single performance would seal their fame and fortune forever. Everyone was very excited.

In the front boat, Jack, Angus, Fanshawe, and the others were all squashed together like sardines, and the rowers made slow progress. They passed Lambeth Palace on the left of the river and on the opposite bank, Westminster Abbey and Westminster Hall. As they made their way slowly upstream, the scene on each side of the riverbank became more rural, with the boatyards and villages increasingly punctuated with open fields, farmsteads, and woodland.

Jack reflected again on what had happened the evening before. Their arrival had saved the day, and as a result they had made themselves instantly popular among the Henslowe Players. The group seemed amused by Jack's and Angus's strange accents and language— but they were used to mixing with and performing in front of all sorts of people, so it didn't seem to bother them too much. There were about twenty actors in the group but even so, a number of them would need to double up on parts for *The Spanish Tragedy*. They were all friendly and welcoming—although there was one, Christo, who seemed a little quieter than the others. Perhaps he only seemed that way because all the others, by contrast, were excessively loud.

After a boisterous dinner, they had slept in claustrophobic accommodation next to the Rose, provided by Henslowe for a fee. There was not room for all of them in the main dormitory, and Jack had ended up in a small alcove next to Christo. He had been furtive and uncommunicative. It had been cold and uncomfortable and Jack had struggled to sleep. After a while, presumably assuming Jack was asleep, Christo had gotten out of his makeshift bed on the floor, lit a small candle, and removed a heavy, ornate cross from his neck, and then held a Bible in front of him. He prayed and chanted for what seemed like an eternity. Even though Christo's voice had been quiet, his words were uttered with passion. Jack could not make out the words, but he could make out the language. Most of it was in Latin, but some of it was in Spanish.

Their last berth before Hampton Court was at Kingston, where they stopped for a leisurely midafternoon lunch before reboarding for the final stretch. The owner of the Swan was delighted to see them, and they all piled inside the small pub on the lower level. A fire crackled away in a large fireplace at one end of the pub. After nearly a day on the river, it was a welcome sight. Soon Henslowe and Alleyn were ordering food and drink and everyone was settling down.

"I'm bursting. Where do you think the luxurious facilities are?" Jack asked Angus. They had become accustomed to limiting trips to the bathroom—first because there usually wasn't one, anyway; and secondly, if there was, the experience was too awful to imagine.

"No doubt a hole in the ground around the back somewhere. Be sure to take your gas mask."

Jack wrapped himself back up in his cloak and disappeared outside again. The Swan was located at the upstream end of the town of Kingston, and at the back of the inn was a large yard that led to a road, partly shielded by some large oak trees. The yard was home to three goats and a number of hens that pecked at invisible specks in the mud. Toward one side a narrow platform was built over a stream that ran into the river. The structure supported three crude wooden huts. The setup was luxurious compared to what Jack had experienced in London, and he hurried inside the first hut, trying not to touch, smell, or look at anything.

As he made his way back to the pub a few minutes later, he saw a carriage with two horses pull up just outside the gates to the yard. At the same time he watched Christo emerge from the inn and scurry across the yard toward the carriage. The door of the carriage opened and a cloaked figure stepped down from the carriage to meet Christo. The man carried a walking stick and was limping. Jack recognized him immediately—Pendelshape.

Jack dived behind a pile of logs. From his position he could just spy Christo in deep discussion with Pendelshape. From time to time Christo would glance back at the inn furtively. In less than two minutes the conversation was over. Pendelshape hauled himself back into the coach, and it rumbled off.

Jack waited behind the logs until the carriage disappeared and Christo had gone back inside, and then he returned to the pub. The late lunch was in full swing and, encouraged by the landlord, Alleyn, Fanshawe, and the rest of the Henslowe Players were taking turns making speeches, singing songs, or reciting poetry to a growing crowd of onlookers. Jack sidled over to Angus, who had moved over to the fire and was watching and applauding along with the rest of the group.

"Find it?" Angus said.

"Yes, and that's not all I found."

"What?"

Jack whispered out of the corner of his mouth, "Pendelshape was just here."

Angus gasped. "What?"

"Shhh." Jack looked around the inn, checking out Christo in particular. "Yeah. But he's gone. Don't look now, but he met him." Jack nodded at Christo, who was ignoring the fun and games in the inn completely and staring thoughtfully out of the window.

"Pendelshape met Christo . . . and then just left?" Angus whispered in amazement. "But . . . he might have seen us. . . . He might know we're here."

"I don't think so. It was as if they had planned to meet. As if Pendelshape knew that the troupe would be stopping here. And I kept an eye on Christo and I don't think he said anything to Pendelshape."

"Well, that's a relief. Close call, though." Angus said.

"Last night when we were freezing our butts off in that pigsty that Henslowe put us up in . . ."

"At least you only had to share with one—I had to share with about ten of them."

"Anyway, I couldn't get to sleep. . . . Christo thought I was sleeping, and he got up to pray."

"So? Maybe he couldn't sleep either—I don't blame him with the amount of snoring and farting going on."

"Yeah, but he is a Catholic. Not that unusual in itself, but I heard him saying stuff to himself—*in Spanish*."

"So?"

"Come on, Angus, keep up. A Spanish Catholic in the Henslowe Players has just had a secret meeting with Pendelshape . . ." Jack said slowly. "Who we know wants to use an existing plot to kill the Queen and create civil war in England, so the country will be ripe for invasion . . ."

"So you're saying that maybe Christo is part of the plot?"

"Exactly, using the Henslowe Players as a cover. But I just don't get it. The Queen is surrounded by bodyguards and soldiers. Even if he was some sort of fanatical killer, I can't see how he could do it on his own."

"Unless Pendelshape has already worked out some way to help him when we get to the palace; you know, some sort of trap."

Jack stared into the fire with a furrowed brow. "Yeah, maybe you're right."

Word had gotten out about the arrival of the Henslowe Players, and the spontaneous party at the Swan had drawn an enthusiastic crowd of locals from Kingston seeking to enjoy the impromptu entertainment. Unfortunately, the quality of the performances was declining rapidly as the Henslowe Players became increasingly inebriated. Nevertheless, the owner was so delighted with his takings and the promise from Henslowe that they would stop again on their return trip from the palace that he donated an entire barrel of Mad Dog and, unbelievably, a live pig to the group.

They tottered back down the pier to the waiting boats significantly worse for the wear. If anything, the boats seemed even more cramped and top-heavy than before—particularly the front one, to which the barrel of ale and the pig were added. The pig seemed to be extremely unhappy with the whole idea and squealed noisily as it was manhandled aboard and tethered between two of the posts that held up the awning. Finally, they were all aboard, and with a great cheer ringing in their ears from the large crowd that had gathered to see them off, they cast off into the river for the final haul up to Hampton Court.

It only took three minutes before the barrel of Mad Dog had been cracked open and the first round distributed in large earthenware tumblers. Five minutes later the singing started, and a mere twenty minutes after that there was the first man overboard. This caused enormous hilarity. It did not seem to occur to anyone that, with the water temperature hovering not far above freezing, the man was lucky to be pulled out alive. He didn't seem to care—a dry cloak and a fresh mug of Mad Dog seemed to be sufficient for him to forget the experience altogether. At the back of the boat, even the pig was offered a mug of Mad Dog to quiet it down. It showed its disdain by squealing louder than ever and then promptly defecating—mostly on Alleyn's shoes, which nearly caused Kyd and Henslowe to fall out the boat themselves, such was their mirth. The whole thing was getting horribly out of control. The boat zigzagged its way unsteadily up the Kingston reach, narrowly avoiding a range of other craft, royal swans, and sundry river life.

The sun was beginning to set as they made their final approach, and immense bands of purple and pink swooped across the darkening sky. To their right the great royal deer park stretched endlessly into the distance, and Jack caught occasional glimpses of deer in the dark shadows between the ancient oaks. A low mist was forming on the river and, in the distance on the right bank, Jack saw the great palace of Hampton Court emerge. Its pink brick had turned a deep crimson in the fading light, and from one of its towers Jack could see the same royal standard he had seen at Fotheringhay—the quadrants of the fleur-de-lis and the three lions. But Fotheringhay Castle had been quite different from this. It was a brutal bulwark of stone built for an earlier, more violent age. By contrast, Hampton Court had a gentler facade—its crenulations and towers were there for show and not for defense. It was a palace and not a castle. A palace fit for a queen.

They drew closer, and the splendid building loomed before them, its presence quelling the drunken blathering. A small group of men scurried from the bank to the pier to help them tether the boats. To mark their arrival, Henslowe was to give a speech of welcome, which had been specially penned by Kyd for the occasion. Although the pig had calmed down a little, it had still found the whole experience highly stressful, and the first priority was to lead it ashore. As the boat glided into its mooring place, Henslowe took up position at the bow, standing pretentiously just behind the little flag emblazoned with the interlinking *P* and *H* of his name, which had been nailed to the prow. The afternoon's revelry had taken its toll on Henslowe as it had with everyone else, and he swayed uneasily on his feet. He held up the paper with his address of thanks to the bemused welcome party who looked on from the landing pier. He cleared his throat and began to speak.

"On this day . . ."

But at that moment, from the stern of the boat, the pig squealed hysterically as it was finally released. Sensing freedom, it scrambled across the baggage and through the passengers at high speed. It then leaped like a large pink missile from the bow of the boat toward the landing stage. Henslowe had no chance. One moment he was there, the next he was flying through the air, dislodged from his precarious position by three hundred pounds of airborne bacon. The pig landed gracefully on the landing stage and slalomed expertly through the surprised onlookers, never to be seen again. Henslowe was not so lucky. He landed with a stylish belly-flop in the river. Everyone in the boat raced to one side to check on the fate of their esteemed leader. The boat was already dangerously top-heavy and the whole thing slued to one side, unbalancing, and then completely capsized. The Henslowe Players, their baggage, and the barrel of Mad Dog (now empty) were all deposited unceremoniously into the Thames.

They had indeed made an entrance at Hampton Court, but it wasn't quite what Henslowe had in mind.

Hampton Court

The recriminations lasted well into the night, and Alleyn, who it turned out had released the pig at just the wrong moment, had nearly walked out in rage at being accused of doing it deliberately. By the morning, however, tempers had improved. Luckily the main props had been fished successfully from the river and the costumes were finally starting to dry out. The two o'clock start time for their performance that afternoon was also approaching, and Jack was impressed by how professionally the Henslowe Players focused on the job at hand.

Their spirits were lifted further when they were led from their quarters through the great courtyards of the palace to where they would be performing: the magnificent Great Hall at the heart of the palace. The hall must have been more than a hundred feet long and sixty feet high, and had a splendid hammer-beam roof. At one end there was a finely carved minstrel gallery and all around there were stained-glass windows and magnificent tapestries. In the oriel window to the right of the dais were the arms of Cardinal Wolsey, the founder of the palace, and in the side windows were the badges and devices of Henry VIII and his wives. At the front and down two sides of the hall a number of cushioned chairs had been laid out in three rows. In the middle, at the front, a throne had been carefully positioned from which the Queen herself would enjoy the inaugural performance of *The Spanish Tragedy*. In the center of the hall a low stage had been erected. Toward the rear of the hall, a screen stretched from one side to the other to mask the actors when they were not performing. Angus, whose duties as stagehand would be complete after setting up, would be allowed to watch the play up in the minstrel gallery.

Two o'clock was approaching fast, and the cast members were limbering up in earnest. The Great Hall was soon a hive of activity. Henslowe manned one of the entrances to the hall, watching nervously for the arrival of the first members of the audience. Kyd fussed from one actor to the next, tweaking costumes and proffering needless advice. Alleyn paced up and down at the far end of the hall in deep concentration, reciting his words to himself over and over again. Even Jack, with his keen memory, had struggled to learn his words in the short time given him. Much of the script was still in Kyd's own extravagant italic handwriting, which was difficult to read. In addition, a number of the spellings and pronunciations were very odd; it had taken him a long time just to understand how Kyd had formed certain letters like the f and s. Kyd had also been inconsistent in how he denoted certain letters, and frequently used two or three different sorts of squiggles to denote the same letter. To complicate matters further, there were whole words Jack just did not recognize or understand. Together, the whole lot was recognizable as English, but only just. Jack was glad that he only had one relatively modest part to learn. Meanwhile, Angus had also been busy. He had spent the morning lugging around the costumes and props, but at last everything seemed to be ready and he sat down next to Jack in one corner of the hall for a final breather before the big performance.

"You ready, then?" he asked.

"I think so."

Jack nodded in the direction of Christo on the other side of the hall. "You been keeping an eye on him?"

Christo fiddled with the cross around his neck. If anything, he had become even more nervous as the time of the performance approached. Nobody but Jack and Angus would have noticed—everyone else was too busy—and anyway, it was normal to look nervous before performing in front of the Queen of England.

"Yes, I swear he's getting more jittery," Angus said.

"That's what I think, too, and I don't like it. He's got to be planning something."

"Seems like it, I know—but what? We were all searched. And

THE

SPANISH TRAGE-

die, Containing the lamentable
end of *Don Horatio*, and *Bel-imperia*:
with the pittifull death of
olde *Hieronimo*.

Newly corrected and amended of such grosse faults as
passed in the first impression.

AT LONDON
Printed by *Edward Allde*, for
Edward White.

Sixteenth-century illustration from The Spanish Tragedy

anyway, he would never get away with it—have you seen the number of guards around the place?"

"I've seen them, but he's up to something and we know that Pendelshape can't be far away—or Whitsun and Gift, for that matter. We need to be ready just—"

At that moment, their conversation was cut short as the large double doors at the rear of the hall flew open. Henslowe had been manning the wrong entrance and missed his big chance to thrust himself in front of the Queen. She swept into the Great Hall surrounded by a large entourage of extravagantly dressed men and women. She wore a stunning white gown embroidered with gold and decorated with precious stones. Around her neck there was a large lace ruff, and her hair was crowned with a ring of bulbous pearls. She had arrived unexpectedly early, walked directly into the backstage area, and taken them all completely by surprise. But it didn't seem to bother her. She marched on, nodding in acknowledgment as everyone turned and bowed.

She took her position on the throne. Soon the Great Hall was packed with other members of her court and every chair was filled. There was a buzz of excitement. This was it. Backstage, Kyd gave a final pep talk as the actors prepared for the performance of their lives, and then the first act of the first public performance of *The Spanish Tragedy* began.

The first act went well. The audience applauded generously, and backstage, Henslowe and Kyd were quietly effusive in their praise. Alleyn and Fanshawe were felt to have done a particularly good job. Much to his relief, Jack had also performed his part to everyone's satisfaction. They needn't have worried about Christo, either. He had performed his role flawlessly and was word perfect. After a short break the second act began, and for the first time on their mad adventure, Jack felt himself relax. He stared up at the extraordinary workmanship of the ceiling of the Great Hall above and the opulence of his surroundings. On the other side of the curtain, the Henslowe Players were starting the second act of *The Spanish Tragedy*—a performance in which Jack himself had just appeared—*in front of Queen Elizabeth I*. The whole thing was utterly extraordinary, and Jack knew that if he thought about it too hard he would go mad . . . or worse, lose concentration, and make some catastrophic slip-up which would somehow doom himself and Angus. He knew they had to keep their wits about them.

He picked up the script and flicked forward to recheck his words for his final short part later on in the play. As he thumbed through the pages, Kyd's italic script flicked past his eyes. Suddenly, one of the pages caught his eye. It was as if he had just had an electric shock. Finally, he understood how Christo planned to assassinate the Queen of England.

A Confusion of Queens

The sword fight, just like the one in *Hamlet,* had already started, and Christo and Alleyn were battling it out onstage in front of an enthralled audience. Jack poked his head around the curtain. Nobody noticed—they were absorbed by the clanging of swords and the acrobatics of the two combatants.

Christo jabbed his sword forward. Alleyn jumped back, but the blade pierced his flesh and instantly an ominous red patch appeared on his billowing shirt. Alleyn glanced down at the wound and looked back up at his opponent, an expression of rage on his face. A frisson of excitement rippled through the crowd. *The Spanish Tragedy* was proving more thrilling than they could have possibly wished for.

Christo's strike found its mark, but Alleyn came back with a violent counterthrust. His blade flashed and caught Christo in the ribs. There was a gasp from the crowd. Then Alleyn darted forward a second time, his sword aimed at Christo's chest. This time Christo swayed to one side, narrowly avoiding the thrust. Christo grabbed his opponent by the arm and heaved him onward while simultaneously thrusting out his leg. Alleyn tripped over Christo's extended leg and spun through the air, landing with a crunching thud on the makeshift stage, his sword spinning from his hand as he made contact. Christo pounced onto his opponent, but Alleyn soon had Christo pinned on his back beneath him. Alleyn grasped Christo's sword hand and banged it hard on the ground until Christo relinquished his grip. Christo was nailed to the ground with Alleyn's bulk pressing down on him. But it wasn't over yet. Christo gritted his teeth, and with a final effort he jerked his knee upward into Alleyn's crotch. He jumped up and snatched a sword. Alleyn grabbed the other sword, and the two of them circled around and around each other, panting like cornered animals. The crowd jeered. There was blood all over the floor, and Alleyn slipped. He was only distracted for a split second but it was enough. Christo leaped forward to land the fatal blow. Alleyn screamed as blood from a second wound spurted from his chest. He dropped to one knee and looked up at Christo before he slumped to the stage floor. Spontaneously, the audience burst into applause.

But now the script changed.

In horror, Jack saw his worst fear unfold in front of him. Christo stepped over the prostrate body of Alleyn in the middle of the stage and marched menacingly toward the Queen, who sat on her throne, enthralled by the spectacle before her. By the time the guards, or the Queen for that matter, realized that Christo's advance was not part of the play it would be too late. From his position on the other side of the stage, Jack could do nothing. Christo was only ten paces away from the Queen and brandished his sword above his head. There was a ripple of unease in the crowd, then Christo dashed forward. Jack screamed out but it was too late. The point of Christo's blade was only six inches from the Queen's throat. She was about to die. But suddenly, Christo simply . . . collapsed. He hit the ground like a sack of potatoes right at the Queen's feet. It was as if he had been shot by a sniper.

It was the next best thing. Up in the minstrel gallery, Angus stood staring down at the scene before him. His catapult hung loosely in one hand. From sixty feet away he had unleashed a missile that had cracked into the back of Christo's head, instantly knocking him unconscious.

The Queen was quickly surrounded by four burly guards brandishing halberds. A number of courtiers drew swords and dragged Christo away. But it wasn't over.

Above them, there was a loud shattering of glass as first one, then a second of the large windows high above them were smashed open. Shards of glass rained into the Great Hall, and Jack narrowly avoided being impaled. At first it was not apparent what had caused the windows to shatter. Then ropes were flung through both windows and two figures abseiled down onto the floor of the Great Hall. They touched down and took up position in the center of the hall, where moments before, Christo and Alleyn had staged their fight. The two men were in sixteenth-century dress, but Jack recognized them immediately: Whitsun and Gift—their Revisionist friends. Both men were holding something close at their sides, disguised by their cloaks. Jack guessed that they must be automatic weapons of some sort. He was so astonished by the arrival of the gate-crashers that he did not really notice the strange reaction of the audience. While members of the cast scurried for cover, the audience was oddly quiet and watchful.

Then Jack witnessed something extraordinary. Before Whitsun or Gift could act or speak, the audience all around the hall dropped to their knees almost as one. It was a perfectly synchronized movement. However, a few courtiers dotted within the audience remained standing, possibly ten or fifteen of them. They were armed with stubby crossbows, which until that point had been carefully hidden.

Whitsun and Gift had no chance. Without warning, the armed courtiers fired. In a moment, the air was thick with deadly bolts released from the crossbows zipping across the hall. Jack watched as the lethal missiles struck home. Whitsun and Gift were peppered. As he dropped to the floor on his knees, Whitsun searched for the trigger of his gun, but a final arrow skewered his neck, and he slumped to the floor. Gift was already prostrate, lying in a growing pool of his own blood, a series of arrows buried up to their feathers in his torso.

The armed courtiers reloaded and stepped forward to take up strategic positions around the hall. Some scanned the windows above, possibly waiting for more armed raiders, others covered the entrances to the Great Hall. Two of them moved toward Whitsun and Gift, who lay center stage—their lifeless eyes staring at the ceiling of the hall. The courtiers leaned down to search and check the bodies. Jack recognized them immediately: Tony and Gordon. They had somehow inveigled their way into the team of armed courtiers who had sprung the trap for Whitsun and Gift.

A door was flung open at the front of the hall, and a tall man with a thin, pale face with a mustache and beard marched in. He was slightly balding, and his dark hair was specked with gray. He had dark, almost black eyes and was dressed in somber black, except for a stiff, white ruff around his neck. Next to him walked a woman. Incredibly, the woman was dressed almost identically to the queen whom Christo had just tried to murder and who now stood up from her throne to curtsy. It was very hard to tell the two women apart. Jack's head was spinning—Whitsun and Gift dead, Tony and Gordon here . . . and now, two queens?

As the second queen entered the Great Hall, everyone turned toward her and bowed. She approached her strange twin and paused briefly. It was uncanny seeing the two women together.

"Lady Sarah, I thank you for your services today." She offered her twin a hand. "Your bravery will be rewarded."

The Queen strode forward to inspect the two prostrate figures of Whitsun and Gift in the middle of the hall. She gave one of them a contemptuous poke with her foot. Tony and Gordon stood nearby, their heads bowed. The hall went quiet as the Queen prepared to speak. Her dark eyes glinted with fiery confidence—a confidence wrought from twenty-nine years of hard-earned power. She spoke clearly and defiantly.

"My friends. We have defeated a plot to murder your Queen—the Queen of England. Let tyrants fear. I have always so behaved myself that under God I have placed my chiefest strength and safeguard in the loyal hearts and goodwill of my subjects, and I thank you for your help in crushing this foul plot. I know I have the body of a weak and feeble woman but I have the heart and stomach of a king, and of a king of England, too, and think foul scorn that Parma or Spain or any prince of Europe should dare to invade the borders of my realm . . ."

The speech continued in a similar vein for some minutes, and when it ended there was a great roar of approval and spontaneously a chant of "God save the Queen" rang out. She stood, chin high, imperious and triumphant. It took several minutes for the adulation to die down. The Queen turned to the dark-clothed man and said quietly, "Walsingham—I trust you will deal with matters now." With that she marched from the hall, surrounded by her escort and followed by her twin—Lady Sarah.

Walsingham took charge. He pointed down at Christo. "The Spaniard, put him in chains. He will be tortured until we know the identities of all the other plotters." He pointed at the bodies of Whitsun and Gift, addressing Tony and Gordon. "Make sure they are stripped to find any other evidence. I have a good mind to send their heads to the Spanish court . . . and, now, where is he?"

Walsingham looked around the hall. Angus had come down from his position in the minstrel gallery and had rejoined Jack and the other members of the cast, who huddled together in one corner of the stage, agog at the proceedings taking place in front of them. Walsingham strode over to them. He was a commanding, sinister figure. Tony and Gordon followed close behind. Walsingham eyed the cast of the Henslowe Players and turned his attention to Angus and Jack at the front.

"And you claim that apart from the Spaniard, Christo, the Henslowe Players had no knowledge of the plot?"

Tony looked knowingly at Jack. "Absolutely not. This is confirmed in Marlowe's letter. By waiting and laying the trap here at Hampton Court we knew we would catch any other plotters red-handed."

Walsingham nodded. "Your point is fair . . ." But then he turned angrily toward Angus. "But you . . . smuggling a weapon into the palace . . ."

Jack intervened before Angus could answer. "Sir, a theatrical prop—just like the swords . . ." As he spoke, Jack spotted a knowing smile of approval cross Tony's lips.

"Indeed, sir," Tony continued, "the fact that this young man saw the danger of Christo and acted to save who he thought to be the Queen proves that he had no knowledge of the plot . . . or indeed of the trap we had laid for the plotters."

Walsingham stared at Jack and then back at Angus with beady, black eyes. Jack could almost hear the mind of the Queen's spymaster whirring away, carefully analyzing their statement for any flaws. But at last, Walsingham gave a firm nod.

"Fine. Indeed, more than fine. You and your friends shall be rewarded." His face relaxed, but there was still no hint of a smile.

"After all, today is a day of triumph—a victory for England—and tomorrow we shall celebrate. The Henslowe Players shall be rewarded, and I shall personally commission an extended run of *The Spanish Tragedy*."

It took a while for it to sink in, but then the Henslowe Players started to cheer and whoop in excitement, and it took no further encouragement for Trinculo to launch into a wincingly bad celebratory jig.

Satisfied, if somewhat perplexed by the reaction of the Henslowe Players, Walsingham moved off to deal with more pressing matters. Tony and Gordon sidled up to Jack and Angus.

"Well, gentlemen, it is good to finally meet up with you again. . . ."

"Likewise, but I think you might have some explaining to do," Jack replied.

"Of course. But first we need to deal with our next problem."

"What's that?" Jack asked.

But Tony did not have time to respond. The doors at the front of the hall flew open and a royal guard hurried over to Walsingham. He looked terrified.

"The Queen! She has been taken. Lady Sarah, too . . ."

Walsingham's face creased up in confusion and shock. "What do you mean?"

The guard stammered, "A man . . . with pistols, he surprised us, killed the other escorts . . . he has taken them"—he waved a hand around his head—"into the gardens."

Walsingham unleashed a sort of primeval scream and then lashed out violently with the back of his hand. He connected with the face of the wretched guard—the blow was so ferocious that his nose exploded in a bloody mess.

"Idiots!" Walsingham started to bark orders. "Secure the gates, secure the water gallery, search the gardens and deer park . . ." He swiveled around to Tony and Gordon. "You—help them!"

Tony turned to Jack and Angus. "As I was about to say, we need to deal with our next problem."

But Jack already understood. "Pendelshape."

Into the Wilderness

Jack, Angus, Tony, and Gordon raced down the steps into the gardens. It was getting dark—a crimson sun was setting in a clear winter sky above the oaks of the deer park. The place was crawling with guards, many with flaming torches above their heads.

They paused for breath at the bottom of the stairs as Tony surveyed the great gardens.

"Pendelshape has managed to kidnap the Queen and Lady Sarah?" Jack asked.

"It must be him . . . desperate to make sure the plot didn't fail," Tony replied.

"Why not just kill her immediately?" Angus said.

"He must have some other warped plan," Gordon said. "And there's something else." He put his hand inside his jacket and took out his time phone. He snapped it open, and the telltale yellow light blinked back at them. "We're getting a time signal."

"We've only got minutes to find him. . . ." Tony looked out at the broad vista of the gardens and the deer park beyond and added in frustration, "He could have gone anywhere!"

Just as the words left Tony's mouth an image popped into Jack's head. It was something from the book that Miss Beattie had shown him. He couldn't have looked at the page for more than five seconds as he leafed through it, but miraculously it now reappeared in his memory, perfectly formed.

"Maybe he's hiding somewhere, waiting for a signal," Gordon said.

Jack knew the answer. "On the outskirts of the palace there is a sort of forest—I'm sure of it."

The others turned toward him. He repeated it: "I think they call it the wilderness—it's a woodland with paths, hedges, and thickets. I remember it from Miss Beattie's book. It's the perfect hiding place, and it's just on the edge of the palace grounds. If we move quickly, we might catch them before they go too far."

The light from the sky was fading fast as they sprinted away from the palace. Soon they were working their way along a narrow pathway to the threshold of the wilderness, the huge trees looming over them. As they made their way through the forest, Jack and Angus became separated from the group. By the time they reached the edge of the forest, they couldn't quite see where the others had gone.

"Which way?"

"No idea."

"That way then . . ." Angus chose one of the pathways.

Occasionally they could hear shouts or orders in the distance as the guards kept up a desperate search in the fading light. Jack and Angus pressed on, taking random turns here and there. Five minutes later, they were utterly lost.

"Stop for a minute." Jack said. "Shall we try and go back?"

Suddenly, they heard a loud scream. It was close.

"What the hell was that?"

"I don't know, but I'm not hanging around to find out."

Jack felt himself starting to panic. They ran on, weaving their way through the trees, and then suddenly found themselves in an oval-shaped clearing, surrounded by thickets and high hedges.

Jack stopped dead in his tracks. The Queen and Lady Sarah stood directly ahead of them with their backs pressed up against a huge oak tree on the far side of the clearing. A man stood in front of them, his pistol leveled at the two women. There was sufficient light from the torches for Jack to recognize Pendelshape instantly. He was pointing the gun at the Queen and then moved it slowly toward Lady Sarah. He seemed to be hesitating, confused by the likeness of the two women.

The arrival of Jack and Angus took him by surprise. He swiveled around and, in panic, fired, but missed. Lady Sarah screamed, and Jack and Angus dived for cover behind a thicket on the edge of the clearing.

Pendelshape shouted out at them, "You have interfered for the last time!"

He fired again but Jack and Angus were well hidden in the thick foliage. Beside himself with frustration, Pendelshape let loose two more shots, but again they went wide. Swinging the gun back toward Lady Sarah and the Queen, he fired again. This time he could not miss. As Jack peered out from the foliage, he saw Lady Sarah's legs give way, and she collapsed in a heap. Something inside Jack snapped. He felt a visceral anger well up inside him. He pounced forward, but as he did so, Pendelshape pressed his gun to Elizabeth's head. She stared back, head high, jaw clenched, eyes defiant. Pendelshape pulled the trigger. Nothing. The magazine was empty. Pendelshape screamed in frustration and fumbled for a fresh magazine, but he was too slow. Jack, enraged by the brutal murder of Lady Sarah, leaped up and crashed into Pendelshape's rib cage at full tilt, lifting him clear from the ground and propelling them both forward before crunching back to the earth. Pendelshape's gun flew free.

Angus, now also up on his feet, looked on with a mixture of dumb-founded astonishment and admiration. Jack was really no match for the stocky and powerful Pendelshape. The teacher had been caught by surprise, but he was quick to recover. Enraged, he lashed out with a clenched fist, which caught Jack square on the side of the head. Jack spun sideways, and the world went dark.

"Time you learned . . . meddling idiot!" Pendelshape growled. He started to crawl around on the ground, cursing angrily and desperately searching for his weapon.

Suddenly, there were voices. Angus shouted, "Help! Over here, we're in the clearing."

A second later, Tony, Gordon, and several other royal guardsmen ran into sight.

"Over there!" Angus pointed at Pendelshape, who was still scrambling around desperately trying to find his gun.

Tony called out to him, "It's over, Pendelshape."

Pendelshape screamed back, "That's what you think . . . VIGIL is about to be crushed!"

"Stand still—or we'll shoot." Gordon shouted.

But Pendelshape was having none of it. He stood up, put his head down, dropped his shoulder, and charged directly through the perimeter hedge. Instantly, Tony and Gordon let loose a volley of shots. For a second all was quiet. Suddenly, there was a flash of incandescent white light, and for a moment the sky above them was as bright as day. Tony and Gordon rushed over to the hedge through which Pendelshape had escaped.

Tony cursed under his breath. "He's gone. Time signal . . . This means trouble. We need to get to the safehouse." He turned back to the guards. "You men, take the Queen and Lady Sarah back to the palace immediately. We will go ahead and track down the intruder. When you get back to the palace, get Walsingham to send help and search the surrounding area. Now, go!"

Tony peered down at Jack. "Are you okay?"

Jack was starting to come around. His head was spinning; he felt like he'd been hit by a bus.

"What happened?"

"You just saved the Queen's life."

Jack just about had the wherewithal to reply, "But not Lady Sarah's?"

Tony grimaced, "Don't know—she's in a bad way . . ."

"We've got to go . . ." Gordon said urgently. "We don't know what Pendelshape is going to do. We need to act while this time signal lasts. We've got a couple of hours at most—come on!"

The guardsmen were already escorting the Queen away from the clearing. But as they prepared to leave, she walked over to where they stood. Her voice trembled with emotion.

"Sir, you have saved my life. I must now return to the palace for protection until the area is secured. Report to us tomorrow, and you shall be rewarded."

"Your Majesty, we must give chase . . . the intruder . . ." Tony pressed.

"Yes, you must go." Then quite spontaneously, she slipped a ring from her finger and pressed it firmly into Jack's hand. "Take this as a token of our thanks. Now Godspeed." She paused before adding grimly, "And when you find the assassin, kill him—and bring me his head."

Day of Deliverance

It took them fifteen minutes to reach what Tony called the safehouse—a hunting lodge that they had already commandeered in the middle of the deer park about a mile from the palace. Jack's head was throbbing from where Pendelshape had punched him and in the dark he had to be supported by Angus and Gordon as Tony led the way through the woodland at a lung-bursting pace. When they had entered the lodge, Jack and Angus were surprised to find a third member of VIGIL waiting for them—Theo Joplin.

"We've got a problem," Tony said.

"I noticed—the time signal," Joplin replied.

"Yes, it all went according to plan, except for one thing—Pendelshape has escaped. He could be anywhere."

Angus was not listening and instead was looking at an array of bags and equipment stacked up against one wall of the room. "What is all that stuff?"

"Weaponry of various sorts. Provisions. When Joplin came back to reinforce us, VIGIL supplied what we needed to defeat Pendelshape. Don't worry about it just now," Tony said.

Jack's head was spinning. "I need to sit down."

"Sorry, Jack—sit there." Tony pulled out a chair. "Gordon, get the kid an ice pack and break out some of the emergency provisions. We'll all need our blood sugar up. We haven't got much time, but let's get ourselves properly organized. What we do next—well, it's life or death now."

Soon they were all sitting around the table inside the main room of the lodge. Joplin had warmed up some tomato soup, and they were working their way through bread, cheese, and chocolate bars. Jack held the ice pack to his head, which still throbbed. Despite this he was listening intently as the VIGIL team quickly pieced together the events of the last few days to work out their next move.

"So, the first Taurus transfer went wrong?" Angus said.

"It dumped us in some godforsaken bog north of London. At that point we didn't know where you two were—you could have been dead," Tony replied. "We had to lie low and wait for the next signal. To begin with, we froze our butts off in some shack, but then we reckoned we should head to London because if you or the Revisionists were going to be anywhere, it was going to be there."

Gordon added, "And finally, we got a time signal. VIGIL located the time phones and identified where you were and where we were—and told us how we could find you. They also sent Joplin back to help us. Luckily going to London was the right move—we were only an hour from your location."

"The torture chamber in that big house?"

"Yes. But we got there too late. We must have arrived after Pendelshape took you away. But then we had our first piece of luck—that letter. Pendelshape made a mistake. In his rush to take all those time phones and take you prisoner, he just left it there, lying on a table."

Jack nodded. "You're right; now that I think about it, I remember him saying he had mislaid it . . . but I don't think he knew he had left it behind."

"What did it actually say?" Angus asked.

"Well, now you know," Joplin replied. "It explained the Spanish plot in detail. One of the plotters, Christo, who was already a member of the Henslowe Players, would use the cover of the visit of the players to Hampton Court to assassinate the Queen. The rest of the letter had details of how various other plotters would encourage sympathetic Catholic aristocrats around the country to rise up on news of the Queen's death and provoke a civil war."

Tony continued, "We disguised ourselves as loyalists who had stumbled across the plot and immediately went to Walsingham."

"Ironically, that was just what Marlowe had asked Fanshawe and us to do," Jack said.

Day of Deliverance

"Interestingly, Walsingham already knew that something was afoot—he had his suspicions of Marlowe, and that's why he was starting to use him as an agent. Marlowe wrote the letter and was torn as to whether he should send it. Then he gave it to Fanshawe, and it miraculously found its way to Walsingham after all. The letter was the last piece of the puzzle. Walsingham moved quickly and decided to set a trap for the plotters at Hampton Court on the opening day of the play."

"The plan worked well," Tony said. "Although, Angus, what you did was a surprise. Gordon was about to take out Christo but you were just too quick."

"But . . . who was that other queen, you know Lady Sarah?" Jack paused, his voice quiet. "Will she die?"

"I don't know. I'm afraid it is likely. She was incredibly brave to act as the Queen's double," Tony replied. "It's a technique that is sometimes used to protect heads of state and VIPs. Lady Sarah looks quite like the Queen . . . and dressed up in all that garb and in character presiding over the play, how on earth was Christo to know any different? It's not as if he'd ever seen a photo of the Queen. In the wilderness it also confused Pendelshape—probably bought some time."

"And the crossbow men?"

"Royal guards, disguised as courtiers. The entire thing was a setup: the whole audience, the Queen's double, everything—we didn't have much time, but it came together."

"You knew that Whitsun and Gift would be there?"

"We were pretty sure, and we hoped Pendelshape would be there as well, together with any other Revisionists, so we could get them all at the same time. The Revisionist plan was to piggyback on the existing Spanish plot. They wanted their interventions to be as 'light touch' as possible—saves them work and makes it all cleaner."

"You and the crossbow men were ready," Angus said. "Brilliant."

"Losing Pendelshape was not so brilliant. Unless we can nail him, we're done for."

Joplin looked at Jack, concentrating hard. "Jack, after Pendelshape took you prisoner, was there anything, anything at all, that he said about his plans to change history?"

"It was pretty amazing. He showed us a kind of game where Spain conquers England and then all of the Americas and that becomes a basis for some sort of global domination. He said there was a way of measuring how it would be better than our present history. Called it UI or something."

"Utility Index?" Joplin looked at his colleagues with ashen-faced incredulity. "They must have developed the causal modeling to a very sophisticated degree . . . very worrying."

"Er, sorry?" Angus said.

Joplin explained, "If this software can really model intended changes into the future with such precision—that is a truly powerful ability. It is a capability that we in VIGIL certainly never thought could be possible. The Revisionists will play God."

"Sometimes I reckon Pendelshape thinks he is God," Jack said.

Joplin rubbed the back of his neck. "This is very serious. Jack, did Pendelshape say anything else—was he more specific about their plans?"

Jack thought for a moment about what Pendelshape had told them. "He said that ideally he needed to do two things. First, he said Elizabeth must die to create disorder across the country—a sort of power vacuum. Then he said the Spanish Armada needed to succeed. The Spanish troops under the Duke of Parma in the Netherlands could then just walk in and take control. In fact, he seemed to think that even if they didn't manage to kill the Queen, the second part of the plan could still succeed, as long as the Armada was successful."

"The Armada—did he say anything more about that?"

Angus piped up, "He mentioned a battle. . . . Grave—something."

Joplin banged the table. "Gravelines! I knew it. That confirms it." Joplin jumped to his feet and started to pace around the room. "I have been piecing together a theory based on the information your father gave us and our knowledge of history. Gravelines was a sea battle that took place in the east of the English Channel during the Armada. The defeat of the Armada came down to many things . . . but if there was one point where you wanted to make a decisive change in favor of the Spanish fleet, Gravelines would be it. Gravelines was the point where the English ships took on the great ships of the Armada. After Gravelines, the Armada fled up the English coast—badly battered but still intact. After that point, though, the storms got them. Those few that did survive the wrecks and struggled ashore were often murdered and robbed. If you were going to change all that for Philip II and Spain, you could probably do it at Gravelines. It would be Spain's day of deliverance."

"How would you do it? I mean—how can Pendelshape on his own take on all those English ships?" Jack asked.

Joplin shook his head. "I don't know. But you're right, Jack, you would need some way to destroy the English fleet quickly and easily. Some form of military superiority. With the fleet at the bottom of the Channel, London and England would be open for the Armada to transport the Duke of Parma's Spanish troops from the Netherlands into England, just as they planned. England's army couldn't resist them. It would only be a matter of a few weeks before all of England was in Philip II's hands. Your information corroborates what we hypothesized: Gravelines is now likely to be the critical date—I am convinced that the Revisionists will use this time signal to stage an intervention. Pendelshape will want to get on with it." Joplin gestured at the bags of equipment arranged along one wall of the room. "We need to get going—let's take what we need. Tony, you need to code the time phone for the battle of Gravelines—August 8, 1588."

"OK." Tony opened a thin briefcase on the table and took out two time phones. He handed one to Jack and one to Angus. "Yours—and don't lose them this time."

Jack picked up the time phone. "Hold on, you're expecting us to come?"

"Of course. It's like Inchquin said—you two are full members of VIGIL—part of the team . . . and where we're going, we're going to need all the help we can get."

"What—you're taking us into a war zone?"

"No mistake, Jack—this is war."

Gravelines
Graveyard

Jack and Angus were squashed into a wooden barrel, which was open at the top. Above them was clear sky. Jack popped his head over the edge of the barrel and immediately wished he hadn't. They were suspended over a hundred feet in the air above a choppy, gray sea. Seconds ago, before the time transport, they had been in the safe-house. The barrel swung in a giddy arc from side to side. It felt like they were on some sort of fairground ride. Instead, they were in a crow's nest soaring high above the deck of the *Revenge,* Sir Francis Drake's flagship, as it led the English line toward the Spanish Armada. The ship's motion in the water was transmitted through the masts so that at the crow's nest the movement was massively accentuated. Jack's response was to cling onto the edge of the barrel to avoid being flung into the abyss below. But his terror was replaced by goggle-eyed incredulity when he surveyed the scene beneath them.

"What is this?"

The sea around them was thick with ships of all shapes and sizes—massive galleons, barges, and hulks. Some were powered by sail, some by oars, and some by both. Everywhere, they could see the white canvas of sails billowing in a freshening wind and a forest of masts, fighting tops, and the complex tracery of rigging. The sails of the great Spanish galleons were emblazoned with giant red crosses. Behind them, the English ships were adorned with crosses of Saint George, the royal standard, and the rose of the House of Tudor.

"Ships . . . everywhere . . ." Angus stuttered in amazement.

"The Battle of Gravelines. Look there . . ."

A scene from the Battle of Gravelines

Jack pointed to a very large Spanish galleon—they could just make out the lettering on its side—*San Martin,* the Spanish flagship. With its raised castles, fore and aft, it towered over the *Revenge,* which by contrast was built for speed and agility. They were close enough to see men with muskets and harquebuses in the fighting tops of the *San Martin* and lines of close-packed soldiers along the rail of the decks ready to fire. Jack knew that the Spanish wanted to grapple and board the English ship, but the Spaniards had already learned from earlier, bitter experience on the Armada campaign that the English would not allow them to do so. Instead, using their greater maneuverability, the English would keep just out of grappling distance, and one by one they would pick off and pulverize each lumbering Spanish galleon with superior gunnery, like a pack of hungry wolves descending on a helpless, tethered cow.

"What are we going to do?" Jack said, his voice cracking in panic.

"Hang on . . . looks like we're going in."

The *Revenge* was less than fifty yards from the *San Martin* when first her bow guns and then her broadside guns erupted in cannon fire. Although Jack and Angus were above the main action, they were still in danger, but the spectacle had a hypnotic momentum, and they stared in wonder as they inched past the *San Martin.* Jack could see that already there were holes in her sails, and some of her magnificent carpentry had been reduced to matchwood. They could hear screaming from the close-packed decks and upper works—the terrible toll of the 'murthering fire' of chain shot, hail shot, and cube shot—each designed to maim, kill, and destroy in its own unique, bloody way.

Jack looked away and instead tried to focus on his feet inside the barrel, but Angus continued to stare—his face lined in horror.

"Jeez. Those poor guys . . ."

Finally, the *Revenge* drifted clear, but the plight of the *San Martin* was not over. Behind them, the rest of Drake's squadron, followed by Frobisher's squadron headed by the *Triumph* and Hawkins's squadron in the *Victory,* lined up in turn to pummel the *San Martin.* They now saw other ships of the Armada rallying to protect the *San Martin,* but the English cannons pounded relentlessly—a progressive rumble as the cannons fired successively along the length of each ship.

Suddenly, a round of chain shot from a Spanish ship spun through the upper rigging of the *Revenge*. It hit the upper mast and sliced through the rope that tethered the crow's nest. Jack and Angus felt the barrel lurch violently as the securing ropes fell away. The barrel inverted itself, although somehow it remained hanging by a single thread. Jack and Angus could do nothing to save themselves, and they slid out of the upturned barrel. Angus was propelled through empty space, but before he could reach any speed, he slammed into a cross-bar, which broke his fall. He clawed desperately at a flapping rope secured from the mast above, which he finally managed to reach and cling to. But then a second shot shredded the crossbar, which promptly collapsed, leaving Angus suspended in the rigging, eighty feet up, swinging from side to side like a human pendulum.

Jack was luckier—but not much. As he was launched deck-ward, the furious assault from the Spanish ship dislodged the upper gallant, and its huge billowing sail floated seaward like a giant parachute. Jack, accelerating rapidly through the air, landed square on top of the rolling canvas as it floated down. The sail deposited him gracefully on the foredeck of the *Revenge* before folding in on itself and floating gently into the sea. Jack had no time to reflect on his incredible escape. The deck of the *Revenge* was alive with men fighting for their lives. He craned his neck upward, searching the rigging for any sign of Angus—but he could see nothing.

"You, there!" a man shouted. "Gun deck!"

With no time to think, Jack found himself being bundled below. The gun deck was a single, low-ceilinged cavern. The massive trunks of the ship's masts passed directly through it—rising from the floor and up through the roof. Inside the gun deck, Jack could see that every timber was black with spent powder. There were huge iron guns decorated with coats of arms, which rested on massive carriages held on wheels cut from whole sections of tree trunk. The oak planking around them was grooved where the guns had been run in and out time and again. Piles of shot and cartridges of black powder were stacked in the lockers by the guns alongside ramrods, powder scoops, and match cord. Suddenly, a cannonball from a Spanish ship ripped though the planking of the gun deck, unleashing a blizzard of splinters. Jack saw one man collapse—impaled by a shard of wood. But his comrades kept grimly to the routine of their work. As the men sweat, the master gunners barked orders. It was a scene from hell, and Jack knew that if he stayed he would die. Nobody noticed as he bolted back up to the deck.

But the deck of the *Revenge* was more nightmarish than the scene below. Jack gagged on the smell of gunpowder, which was heavy in the air. The smoke from the guns cloaked the water in great billows of dark mist, causing ships to appear and disappear like hulking beasts. Bodies of the injured and dying lay across the deck of the *Revenge,* but it was nothing compared to the damage to the Spanish ships. Some ships were close, and Jack could see that their sails were tattered and torn and their decks splintered and strewn with the dead—blood pouring from the scuppers as they heeled in the wind.

"Down here!"

Jack swiveled. Angus!

"How did you . . . ?"

"Never mind about that—I found the others. Come on!"

Jack followed Angus into the aftcastle of the *Revenge* and down into the captain's cabin. It was strewn with broken furniture, books, and the half-empty bags from the safe house. Tony was near the shattered rear windows wrestling with some sort of large tubular device. To one side, Joplin knelt beside a prostrate Gordon, who groaned in pain.

"What happened to him?" Jack said.

"Gun shot—got him in the shoulder," Joplin said. "Keep your heads down—the cabin has already been hit twice."

"Is he going to be OK?"

"Think so—if we can get him home quickly while we still have the time signal"—Joplin nodded toward Tony—"but you two need to help over there. We've got a problem."

Then Jack heard it. Over the sound of the cannon, gunfire, and cries of sailors, they could hear the shrill whine of an aircraft engine and a loud mechanical whirring. Jack and Angus peered gingerly through the windows at the rear of the captain's cabin. Emerging from the billowing clouds of gun smoke, a black military helicopter appeared, hovering a mere thirty feet above the water. The machine was utterly incongruous with the great sailing ships of the Armada.

Joplin had said that Pendelshape would require a decisive military advantage to defeat the English fleet and give the Spanish the naval superiority they would need to stage the invasion of England. It was now clear how that advantage would be achieved and how the Armada would snatch victory from the jaws of defeat. In a final throw of the dice, Pendelshape was about to give Philip II his day of deliverance and change the course of history forever.

"What is *that*?" Jack said.

"Helicopter gunship," Tony said. "Pendelshape and the Revisionists have transported it back on the time signal. We got here at the right time."

"It's a *what*?"

"A Westland WAH-64 Apache—British Army version. It's got the Rolls-Royce engines. And a chain gun that will fire over six hundred rounds a minute. And those pods on the side carry hellfire and CRV7 rockets. It's a beast," Angus said in admiration.

"Never mind that—Pendelshape is inside with a copilot and God knows what else and we haven't got much time before he takes out the whole of the English fleet—and us with it. *So, help me!*"

Jack and Angus looked at the strange device that Tony wrestled with as he spoke. It looked like a fat steel tube. There was a large sight attached to the top and a trigger underneath.

"What is that thing? Looks like a bazooka."

"It's a Man-PAD," Tony said.

"Is that a real word?"

"Does it really matter?" Tony replied in frustration. "A Man Portable Air Defense system. One of the toys we brought back with us . . . There," Tony said triumphantly, "We're ready."

Angus nodded through the window. "Well, I hope so, 'cause we have incoming."

The helicopter pirouetted on its vertical axis, sniffing out its first prey. The English flagship seemed a good place to start, and the machine was directly level with the stern of the *Revenge*. Suddenly, the chain gun hanging from its belly exploded into life and bullets ripped into the upper part of the cabin, unleashing a blizzard of splinters over the heads of Jack and Angus, who hugged the floor. Tony was not so lucky. One second he was holding the Man-PAD by the window, the next he was gone—flung from one side of the cabin to the other by a single round from the helicopter gun. He lay on the floor, clutching his upper arm, cursing bitterly. The firing stopped and the helicopter hung in the air, gathering itself for another assault. Jack and Angus rushed over to help Tony.

"Don't worry about me," he said through gritted teeth. "Get him before he kills us all . . ."

Angus rushed back, grabbed the launcher, and heaved it up onto his shoulder. He staggered toward the window, which had been completely obliterated by the storm of bullets. He aimed at the helicopter, closed his eyes and squeezed the trigger.

Nothing happened.

Jack was now at his side, and they could both see the helicopter inching forward for the final kill.

"I think you need to switch it on."

Jack flicked a switch on the side of the launcher, and it hummed into life.

This time Angus kept his eyes open and aimed. He fired and the rocket fizzed from the muzzle of the launcher and smashed into the housing beneath the rotor blades. There was an explosion, but as the smoke cleared, incredibly the helicopter was still there—just hanging in the air.

Jack turned in desperation to Tony at the back of the cabin, "It's still there!"

But then the tone of the engine changed and the rhythmic whirring of the blades seemed to falter. The machine hung for a moment longer and then dropped like a stone into the sea. Jack and Angus looked on as the pilot struggled to free himself from the rising water level inside the cockpit. As he looked down from the stern cabin of the *Revenge,* Jack clearly saw Pendelshape raging at them from inside the cockpit.

Sultan of Spin

Beneath his feet, Jack saw the shimmering eddies of electricity consolidate and then morph into the steel platform of the Taurus. The heavy metal struts that bounded the inner shell of the great machine gradually came into focus, and the features of the control room beyond the thick green glass of the blast screen became clearer. The blast screen was lowered and a number of people in the control center came forward—they were clapping and cheering. Jack blinked. He could see Inchquin, the Rector, Beattie, and, right in front, his mom, beaming from ear to ear. They were home.

Jack and Angus made their way down the gantry from the Taurus and Jack could hear the hum from the generators dying away as they powered down. The medical team rushed forward to help down the injured Tony and Gordon, who were immediately dispatched to the underground hospital. Carole Christie ran to hug Jack, and seconds later Inchquin and then the Rector were shaking their hands. It was over.

Following a medical examination and a meal, they decamped to VIGIL's Situation Room to debrief. The team sat around the same table where Inchquin had chaired the first meeting after hearing the news from Jack's father about his break from Pendelshape. They spent the next few hours picking through their experiences in the sixteenth century—supported by analysis from the rest of the VIGIL team. Jack struggled to get his head around it all.

"So, how do you know that our mission was a success—that we don't have to go back and do any tidying up of anything . . . any impact we had?"

Inchquin smiled. "I know it is difficult to understand, but it is self-evident. We are all still here, and history as we remember it was the same before your mission as it is now—a mere twenty-four hours later . . ."

"But what if Pendelshape had succeeded?" Angus said.

"If the Revisionist mission had been a success we would be living in a very different world and perhaps would not exist at all. Anyway, we think that is the case. The point is, we don't really know for sure, and for that reason alone it is extremely dangerous to meddle in history."

"When we met Pendelshape he said that their modeling techniques were now so sophisticated that the Revisionists would somehow be able to protect themselves from the changes they made—you know, make changes to history so the future was better—but kind of keep them and their Taurus separate . . ." Jack looked at Inchquin with a furrowed brow. "Is that *possible*?"

Inchquin shook his head. "It's called lineage isolation. They clearly *think* it's possible—and it may be perhaps with repeated interventions—but we think that to try such a thing is utter madness."

Jack's brain was working overtime. "By what you're saying, then . . . does that mean we kind of know that the Revisionists will never be successful, because if they had—history would already be different?"

Inchquin smiled. "Very good, Jack. Indeed, that is one theory—that history as we know it already reflects what has happened, including any interventions that the Revisionists have made, and in fact, interventions we have made to stop them."

Angus moaned. "Sorry, I'm lost—this is a complete mind-bender."

"The point is, Angus, much of this time theory is conjecture. However clever the scientists are, we just don't understand it well enough—we are on the edge of the unknown. But our position is clear—the human race is not some sort of experiment in a petri dish to fiddle around with."

"Well, one thing is for sure," Joplin said breezily, "we now know much more about what did happen, including the Player's Plot. It's funny—it just isn't really a big deal in the textbooks."

"What do you mean, Theo?"

"Well, as you know, the plot exists in the historical archive—however, it is practically a footnote. But we know from what we saw at Hampton Court that it was one of the most dramatic of the many plots against Elizabeth in the late sixteenth century. My theory now is that Walsingham suppressed much of the detail—including the death of Lady Sarah."

"Why?"

"Although unearthing the plot and trapping the assassins so brilliantly at Hampton Court was a triumph for England, and a personal triumph for Walsingham, on reflection he clearly decided that the whole thing was too close for comfort—particularly the narrow escape in the wilderness. The Queen might well have died and the kingdom might have been thrown into turmoil. Walsingham must have considered it much better to perpetuate the image of the Faerie Queene—untouchable, inviolate, supreme; you know, all that—rather than publicize the reality of the plot too enthusiastically. . . ."

"No decapitated heads, I guess?"

"Far too unsubtle. And remember Elizabeth's speech in the hall?"

Jack nodded.

"Well, that was reused, of course—it is now remembered as part her famous speech at Tilbury, which was delivered more than a year later, when the threat of the Armada passed."

"Elizabeth—the first sultan of spin." Joplin chortled at his own joke. "I guess she was ahead of her time."

"What happened to Marlowe?"

"A bit of a mystery. We know that the Spanish took him into hiding following the incident in Cambridge. When the plot fell through, there was no evidence for the Spanish to really pin the blame on him. We think that Walsingham continued to use him as a spy, but may have finally lost patience a few years later. Marlowe was murdered—a dagger above the right eye. Some say it was a drunken brawl, but others say that it was an assassination because all three of the other men who were with him when he died worked for Walsingham and his brother."

There was silence for a moment, and for some reason the words from Marlowe's portrait ghosted through Jack's mind:

What feeds me destroys me.

"One thing," Angus said. "What about a helicopter appearing in the middle of the Armada? I've never heard of that before—you're not telling me that Walsingham could have managed to hush that up, too."

Joplin laughed. "Good point. My theory is that there was such confusion during the battle—the smoke, the noise—you saw what it was like—that few people actually even really saw it. Remember, it was only there for a few minutes. Those that did see it, and survived, referred to a 'fiery monster descending into the sea' or 'a lightning bolt from the finger of God'—all explanations that historians readily put down to the religious hysteria of the time or post-traumatic stress disorder suffered by the witnesses. Remember that a lot of the Spanish men died and actually a lot of the English did, too. Anyway, such reports as existed were felt to be nonsense—and were treated as such later on by serious historians."

"But we know better," the Rector said as he stood up and pointed to an electronic map on the wall. "We have already dispatched a salvage crew to the English Channel to determine if anything was left of the helicopter wreck at the bottom of the sea, even though it is now four hundred years after it sank. If we can identify bones or teeth in the wreck, it will prove that Pendelshape and whoever else was in that blasted contraption are gone for good—and with them, hopefully the entire Revisionist cause."

By the time Jack and Angus wearily climbed into Carole Christie's battered old VW Golf, it was nearly midnight.

"I called your parents, Angus, to say you would be late and would sleep over with us tonight," Carole said.

"Thanks." Angus slapped his forehead. "Hey! I nearly forgot."

"What?" Jack said.

"It's the final match of the season tomorrow!"

Taser Town

It was a beautiful spring day. Jack cycled his mountain bike up the old driveway at Cairnfield and then onto the main road, which led up the long hill to High Street. It was a busy Saturday afternoon and the world seemed to be out enjoying the day. Angus was waiting outside Gino's and had a big grin on his face. He saw Jack and waved something in the air. It was the rugby trophy.

"We won!"

"Good stuff—did you score?"

"Just one try." Angus jerked his head toward the café. "Come on—grilled cheese to celebrate, then I've got to head home."

Gino was delighted to see them. In fact he was so delighted that he immediately closed the shop and shuffled everyone else out, making some excuse about a gas leak.

"So some adventure, eh?" He winked at them conspiratorially. "You two big VIGIL heroes now. What can I get you? On the house." He grinned. "Don't tell me: double Gino-chino, extra shot, full fat, with caramel and extra whipped cream . . ." Then Angus and Gino announced in unison, "and don't forget the cherry." Gino thought this was absolutely hilarious, and his belly wobbled as he laughed uproariously.

"Some sandwiches too, please, Gino."

Jack and Angus settled into one of the booths. Angus immediately started fiddling with the large plastic tomato-shaped ketchup holder. He squeezed it so the sauce just oozed out of the top before releasing his grip so that the thick red liquid was sucked back in with a satisfying squelch.

"That's disgusting," Jack said after enduring the third repetition of the procedure.

"Sorry," Angus replied. "Hey, have you still got it? You know, the ring or whatever old Queenie gave you?"

Jack smiled and reached into his pocket. He placed the ring on the table. It glinted up at them.

Angus looked agog at the ring. "It's a whopper. Green—what's that?"

"Emerald, stupid. That's the stone. The ring is gold."

"What do you think it's worth?" Angus said.

Jack shrugged, "Thousands, maybe tens of thousands . . ."

"*Awesome.* Are you going to keep it?"

"Of course. It's mine. Queen Elizabeth I of England gave it to me—the Faerie Queene—I saved her whole kingdom and the human race . . . though granted, you did help," Jack said, smiling.

Angus laughed. "Fair point."

"Hey, I brought something else to show you," Jack said. "Really weird . . . I mean, almost as weird as some of the other stuff we've seen."

Jack pulled out from his bag the large history book that Miss Beattie had loaned him about the Elizabethan era.

"Don't know if you remember this—Beattie gave it to me before we went back. It's got all sorts of pictures and stuff about Queen Elizabeth and the sixteenth century. . . ." Jack thumbed through the pages. "Check that out."

Jack pointed at the small frame at the bottom of one of the pages. It was the one he had noticed before entitled *Elizabethan Troupe*. It was a simple color plate of a group of actors in various costumes. There was one dressed as a court jester and next to him, in stark contrast, another dressed as a monk. There was a third who looked slightly more important—like a country gentleman with a fine cloak and a neat, pointed beard.

"No way!" Angus nearly slid off the vinyl seat. "It's the Marlowe Players at Corpus Christi, and that's got to be Fanshawe, Trinculo, and Monk . . ."

"And?" Jack asked.

Eyeing the picture closer, Angus spotted two further figures off to one side. One was tall and broad with longish black hair. The other was shorter, more slender, and had a shock of blond hair. For a moment Angus could not place them. Then he realized—it was them: Angus and Jack.

"Didn't really notice those two before. But that's not all. There's a painting of the Gravelines battle—you know, with the 'fiery god' shown."

Angus was not impressed. "Doesn't look much like a helicopter to me. Certainly not a WAH-64 Apache armed with a chain gun and CRV7 rockets."

"Well, as Joplin said, that's the problem with eye witness accounts."

"And historians."

"I nearly forgot!" Jack said, pulling out his cell phone. "I got a message. . . ."

"Oh yeah? Who's it from?"

"Dad." Jack said. "Look."

"Angus squinted at the text and read aloud:

Let us go in together;
And still your fingers on your lips, I pray.
The time is out of joint; O cursed spite,
That ever I was born to set it right!

"It's that weird quote again—about the world being broken and someone having to sort it out. Wasn't that what you said?"

Jack smiled. "Sort of—it's a verse from *Hamlet*."

Angus read on.

Jack,
Sources tell me that you have had quite an adventure. I heard about Pendelshape's poorly planned and badly executed attempt to change history. It is not how I would have done it, were I still in charge.

I see now that you are finding your own way
in life, and I understand that it may not be
the way that I have chosen. You have to make
your own choices, Jack. Despite this, I
still hope that we might meet one day to talk
as friends, and perhaps I can even find a way
to make peace with VIGIL.

But what I really wanted to say is this: I
am proud of you.

Dad

Angus looked up. "Wow. What do you think he'll do next?"

Jack shrugged. "No idea. He's in a pretty desperate situation. . . .
Must be tough to be on the run from VIGIL."

Gino brought over the Gino-chinos and the sandwiches and then
took his own place next to them at the booth, a small espresso in front
of him.

"You did very well, boys. The whole team is proud. . . ."

Francesca, Gino's daughter, emerged from the back of the café. She
was burdened with large shopping bags. Gino winced and whispered
to Jack and Angus, "Watch it boys; Francesca in bad mood."

Sure enough, Francesca marched up the aisle between the booths
and dumped the bags at Gino's feet.

"Why am I the only one that does any work around here?" she
demanded.

"Hi, Francesca," Angus said breezily. But his greeting was returned
with a withering stare.

"I'm sick of this pokey little shop, and I'm sick this of this pokey
little town."

Gino looked hurt. "But my dear . . ."

But the girl had clearly had enough. "There's nothing to do
here. . . . Nothing ever happens. . . ."

Day of Deliverance

But Gino's moody daughter could not have been more wrong. Around the booth next to them, there was a disturbance in the air, then a blinding flash of white light. In front of them appeared a tall man with a rich tan and chiseled features. He wore a fine black cloak. Next to him were two shorter, powerfully built men. One had a badly disfigured eye and a scar that stretched from his forehead across the side of his eye and down his cheek. The last time Jack and Angus had seen Delgado, Hegel, and Plato was in the torture chamber just before Jack had tricked them with the time phone and zapped them into hyperspace. Little did he know that they were to be transported to Gino Turinelli's Italian Café in the middle of High Street.

Although they looked dazed and confused, it did not take long for Delgado to gather his wits. He had no idea where he was, but he recognized Jack and Angus and he drew his sword. Francesca screamed. Gino was the first to react. He leaped from the booth and dived over the counter of the café. For a portly man, he moved surprisingly quickly. In an instant Plato was after him, sword in hand. He jumped up onto the counter and swung his sword around his head, dislodging great lumps of plaster from the ceiling and sending plates, glasses, bottles, and jars flying around the café. Gino slowly got to his feet and raised his hands from behind the counter in a gesture of surrender. Plato stopped waving his sword around and, from his position on the counter, lowered it menacingly so it touched the base of Gino's throat. He looked back over his shoulder to Delgado, awaiting orders. Hegel grabbed Francesca from behind and held a dagger to her cheek. Francesca whimpered in fear. Delgado approached Jack and Angus with his sword outstretched.

Jack glanced over at Gino, who was trembling and had his eyes closed. But Jack noticed that in one of his outstretched hands he was grasping something . . . a cell phone.

Delgado hissed at Jack, "Where are we—what kind of *witchcraft* is this?"

Delgado was no longer speaking in the calm and collected way he had done in the cellar. He was confused and scared—dangerous and unpredictable.

"You speak, my friend." He glanced over at Hegel, who pressed the flat side of his knife to Francesca's cheek. "Or the girl dies."

Suddenly, in the distance, they could hear the sound of a police siren. Jack's heart leaped—somehow Gino had made the emergency call.

Delgado heard the noise, too, and he became more agitated. "What is this noise?"

He left Jack and Angus unguarded for a moment and gingerly crept forward to the plate glass window at the front of the café and peered into the street beyond. The good people of Soonhope, oblivious to the strange events taking place inside the town's favorite Italian café, were going about their business—just like any other Saturday lunchtime. Jack could see the look on Delgado's face as he looked from one end of High Street to the other. It was the same expression of stupid shock Jack must have shown when he regained consciousness on top of the tower at Fotheringhay Castle beneath the royal standard. In one way what Delgado saw was normal—there were people out there with arms and legs—just like him. And there was a large building at one end of the street that looked oddly familiar—a church—a strange relic from his time. But the people were dressed in an extraordinary way. There were no horses or carts. And the place was strewn with large, colored boxes . . . on wheels.

Delgado was still standing paralyzed in front of the window when three particularly distinctive metal boxes arrived—ones with blue and red flashing lights on the top. The people of Soonhope had no time to register that the most exciting event in their town's history was happening right before their eyes. The plate glass window of Gino's café shattered and before Delgado could react the two dart-electrodes from a Taser gun hit him square in the chest, and he screamed as the electric charge coursed through his body. Behind him, Hegel and Plato experienced the same fate as police stormed in from the back of the café. Incapacitated, the three men were quickly bundled into the back of a police van and driven off at high speed. Naturally, VIGIL's reach also extended to the local police force. The café was quickly cordoned off. Soon afterward, Tony arrived—his shoulder heavily bandaged from his injury. He looked around the café. Glass from the smashed front window had sprayed across the floor, and there was broken crockery strewn everywhere. Policemen were inspecting the debris. In one corner, Gino tried to comfort Francesca, who sobbed in his arms. Jack and Angus hadn't budged from their position in the booth.

"I don't know what it is with you two," Tony said. "But you always make such a mess."

The Last Act

Jack knew what he had to do. Clutching his chest to stem the bleeding, he staggered across to where his uncle sat cowering behind the long banqueting table. The food and drink were still laid out, untouched. Jack mounted the table and fixed his eyes menacingly on his uncle, who sank back into his chair, shaking. There was to be no mercy, and Jack did not hesitate—he thrust the sword into his uncle's heart.

Soon, the first performance of *Hamlet* at Soonhope High was over. The audience of parents and locals gave the tired but happy cast a well-deserved standing ovation. As rehearsed, Jack held out his hand to the wings and Miss Beattie came onto the stage, blushing slightly. She did a little bow and was handed a bunch of flowers from one of the cast members. There were calls of "bravo" from the audience. After a few more bows, the curtains closed.

Jack and Angus joined the backstage party to celebrate the success of opening night.

"I'll make an actor of you yet, Angus. . . ." Jack said.

"Think it was watching the Henslowe Players for all those hours."

"Nice of Beattie to give you a chance . . . " Jack looked around the room. "Here she is now, looking pleased."

"And here come the Rector and Inchquin . . ."

"They're out in force tonight."

"And your mom."

In a minute Jack and Angus were surrounded by the Rector, Inchquin, and Beattie.

"Congratulations!" The Rector put out his hand. "A fine performance. You've done the school proud."

"You might have heard, we've had a bit of a crash course over the last week," Jack replied.

Inchquin smiled. "So I hear, Jack, so I hear." He lowered his voice, to ensure that they were not overheard. "Which brings me to another matter. You should know: our salvage team finally found the wreck of the helicopter in the English Channel."

"Oh?"

"Yes. Apparently, all silted up and badly corroded. It's been lying there for four hundred years, after all."

"What about the bodies—any, er, remains of the people inside . . ." Jack asked.

There was a flash of concern on the Rector's face. "No, Jack. We found nobody . . . no one at all."

BACKGROUND INFORMATION

In *Day of Deliverance*, Jack and Angus travel back to 1587 and 1588—late Elizabethan England. The period is one of the most extraordinary in English history. During this time there was a renaissance in the creative arts, war between England and Spain, religious conflict, and the discovery of new worlds. The period is known for a cast of colorful and legendary figures such as Francis Drake, Walter Raleigh, Mary, Queen of Scots, and of course, Queen Elizabeth I. Some people regard these and other people from the time as heroes, but others may regard them quite differently—even as criminals or pirates. The notes below give a little further information on the places and people that Jack and Angus encounter on their journey, including which are real and which are not.

What was the Armada?

The Spanish Armada was a large Spanish fleet that sailed against England in 1588. Philip II of Spain mobilized the Armada because he was a devout Roman Catholic and considered the Protestant Queen Elizabeth I to be a heretic and the illegitimate ruler of England. Philip supported various plots to overthrow Elizabeth and place Mary, Queen of Scots on the throne instead. The execution of Mary, Queen of Scots strengthened Philip's desire to defeat England. Elizabeth supported Protestant interests elsewhere in Europe—particularly in the low countries, where she supported a Protestant Dutch revolt against the Spanish who ruled there. The English also attacked Spanish interests in the New World and the flota—the Spanish treasure fleets—that transported gold and silver across the Atlantic to Spain.

A chart of the Armada's course from Calais and around the coast
of Scotland and Ireland, 1588

Background Information

What was the plan?

The expedition was led by the Duke of Medina Sidonia, who was relatively inexperienced in naval warfare. The Spanish plan was to sail from Spain up the English Channel and rendezvous near Calais with the experienced Spanish army commanded by the Duke of Parma in the Spanish Netherlands. From here, the army would be transported on barges across the English Channel and would invade England. England had no army to compare with Parma's, and it was assumed that conquest would quickly follow. Philip II gained the support of the Pope Sixtus V, who treated the enterprise as a crusade and promised to give money to the cause (but only when it was successful). In the end he paid nothing.

What happened?

The Spanish fleet set off with about twenty warships of the Spanish navy plus a hundred or so converted merchant vessels with about 30,000 soldiers and sailors aboard. They sailed up the English Channel using a defensive crescent formation and were harried along the way by the English navy—which in total numbered around 200 ships. The Armada met its first objective and anchored off Calais. While the Spanish fleet waited for communication from Parma, the English launched a fire ship attack, which caused the Spanish to panic and many ships to cut their anchors. The following day, the English and Spanish navies engaged each other at the battle of Gravelines. Five Spanish ships were lost, and the Spanish fleet headed north along the east coast of England pursued by the English fleet. Many of the Spanish ships at this stage were badly damaged. After this, the Armada became caught up in a series of storms around the north and west of Ireland and this sealed the fate of the Spanish fleet.

What were the losses?

Around twenty-six ships were wrecked off the coast of Ireland, one off the coast of England, and two more off the coast of Scotland. Two ships reached Norway. Approximately half of the Armada's ships never made it back to Spain. By comparison, the English lost no ships.

Around two-thirds of the Spanish personnel died—for every one killed in battle a further six to eight died of execution, drowning, thirst, hunger, disease, or sepsis. Many wrecks were plundered by locals, and the survivors robbed and murdered. English losses were comparatively few but after the victory, disease and hunger killed many English sailors and troops (perhaps as many as eight thousand) when they were discharged without pay. Despite the government's shortage of money, some historians regard this as a blight on Elizabeth and her regime—that the heroes of the Armada were left to die. By contrast Philip II was generous to the survivors of the Armada who made it back to Spain, despite the defeat.

Why did the Armada fail?
It failed for a number of reasons:
1. **Poor leadership, planning, and communication:** For example, there was no coordination between Philip II and his leaders as to how and when the Spanish troops would rendezvous with the Armada off Calais. By contrast, the English fleet included seamen such as Drake, Howard, and Frobisher, who had significant seafaring experience—specifically against the Spanish. That said, the English leaders were motivated both by the prospect of personal gain as well as duty to the Crown.
2. **Tactics and technology:** The Spanish preference, and traditional naval fighting technique, was to use the ship as a platform to grapple or ram and then board the opposing ships. By contrast, the English used coordinated gunnery to attack the opposition without boarding. In fact, in thirty years of naval warfare during this period, no English ship was sunk by Spanish gunnery. English guns were more accurate, had a longer range, and were fired many times more often than the equivalent Spanish guns. As so often is the case in warfare, the decisive advantage came down to the application of superior technology.
3. **Ship design:** English ships had been significantly redesigned by John Hawkins and the first master shipwright Matthew Baker prior to the Armada. They were race built (which comes from the word

raze—they had lower aft- and forecastles); they were longer in the keel and sat lower in the water. This made them faster and more maneuverable.

4. **Home advantage:** The English fought in waters they knew well, and the Spanish ships, when wrecked, found themselves in hostile countries.

5. **The weather:** As the Armada retreated from the battle of Gravelines, it still posed a significant threat. However, many of the ships were badly damaged and many personnel were already suffering from injury, disease, and shortage of provisions. As a result they were poorly prepared to survive the storms that awaited them as they made their way back to Spain.

What happened afterward?

The English victory over the Armada was significant in naval warfare terms, as it confirmed the superiority of gunnery over ramming and boarding. After its defeat, the Spanish navy was reformed and managed to keep control over its home waters and ocean routes well into the next century. In England, the boost to the legend of Elizabeth, national prestige, and the Protestant cause lasted for years. The belief that God was behind the Protestants was shown by medals that bore the inscription, *He blew with His winds, and they were scattered.* However, the Anglo-Spanish War dragged on to a stalemate that left Spanish power in Europe and the Americas largely intact.

Was the Battle of Gravelines a turning point?

It is important to see the Armada as one major event in a succession of conflicts during the undeclared Anglo-Spanish wars which went on between 1585 and 1604. There were other Armadas and indeed the English under Drake conducted a successful raid on Cadiz in Spain in 1587. By contrast, an expedition by Drake the year after the Armada was a miserable failure. Possibly Gravelines was not as significant a turning point as portrayed in *Day of Deliverance,* but the defeat of the Armada certainly boosted England's confidence and naval power. Some historians say that other factors were equally important to Spain's relative decline in the following century. For example, the immense wealth she gained from the New World, ironically, may have actually hampered the development of commerce and trade and parallel innovations such as stock markets (first in the Netherlands and then in England) which helped drive the creation of wealth and power to new levels in those countries.

Who was Elizabeth I?

Elizabeth I was born in 1533 and died in 1603. She was the Queen of England and the Queen of Ireland from 1558 until her death. She was the daughter of Henry VIII and Anne Boleyn and was the last monarch of the Tudor dynasty. One of her first moves as queen was to support the establishment of an English Protestant church. This Elizabethan Religious Settlement later evolved into today's Church of England. Despite several petitions from parliament and numerous courtships, she never married. In government, Elizabeth was more moderate than her father and her predecessors Mary and Edward. Elizabeth was cautious in foreign affairs and only halfheartedly supported a number of ineffective military campaigns in the Netherlands, France, and Ireland. But the defeat of the Spanish Armada associated her with one of the greatest victories in English history.

What was the speech at Tilbury?

In *Day of Deliverance* Elizabeth makes a speech at Hampton Court. This scene, of course, is fictitious, but the words are real and were purported to have been delivered by Elizabeth at Tilbury in Essex in August, 1588, following a triumphant barge trip down the Thames. At Tilbury, 4,000 troops under the Earl of Leicester listened to the speech and cheered their queen—resplendent in a simulacrum of armor and fine jewels. The speech is one of the most famous in English history—a moving declaration of defiance in the face of extreme adversity. But the reality may have been somewhat different. Historians believe that the speech was carefully refined after the event before being published widely. In addition, the speech was made somewhat after the event, when the real threat of the Armada had passed and was already being torn apart by the gales north of Scotland. But Elizabeth was never one to miss a publicity opportunity, and in this sense she was a forerunner of a much more modern type of politician.

Who was Mary, Queen of Scots?

She was Queen of Scots from 1542 to 1567. Mary was born in 1542 and executed, as described in *Day of Deliverance,* at Fotheringhay Castle on February 8, 1587. In 1558, she married Francis, Dauphin of France, who became King Francis II in 1559. After Francis died, Mary returned to Scotland and married her first cousin, Henry Stuart, Lord Darnley four years later. After Darnley's death she married James Hepburn, the Earl of Bothwell, who was generally believed to be Darnley's murderer. Following an uprising against the couple, Mary abdicated in favor of her son, James VI. After an unsuccessful attempt to regain the throne, Mary fled to England seeking protection from her cousin, Queen Elizabeth I. Elizabeth, however, ordered her arrest, because of the threat presented by Mary, who had previously claimed Elizabeth's throne and was considered the legitimate sovereign of England by many English Catholics. After a long period of custody in England, she was tried and executed for treason following her involvement in three plots to assassinate Elizabeth—including the Babington Plot, where she was implicated by her own letters, which Sir Francis Walsingham had arranged to come straight to his hands. From these letters it was clear that Mary had sanctioned the attempted assassination of Elizabeth.

Who was William Shakespeare?

William Shakespeare was an English poet and playwright. He was born in 1564 and died in 1616. Quite simply, he is regarded as the greatest writer and playwright in the English language. He wrote thirty-eight plays, 154 sonnets, and several other poems. His plays have been performed more often than those of any other playwright.

There have been many theories that others wrote Shakespeare's material but it is generally believed by scholars that William Shakespeare is the true author.

Who was Christopher Marlowe?

Christopher Marlowe was an English playwright who was born in 1564 and died in 1593. He attended The King's School, Canterbury, and Corpus Christi College, Cambridge, on a scholarship. There has been speculation that Marlowe was a secret agent working for Sir Francis Walsingham. Marlowe's work includes *Dido, Queen of Carthage; Tamburlaine; the Jew of Malta; and The Tragical History of Doctor Faustus.* His plays were very successful in his time. Marlowe died in suspicious circumstances: He had spent all day in a house in Deptford with Ingram Frizer, Nicholas Skeres, and Robert Poley—all three of whom were employed by either Francis or Thomas Walsingham. Frizer and Marlowe argued over the bill for their drink and Marlowe snatched Frizer's dagger and attacked him. In the ensuing struggle, Marlowe was stabbed above the right eye and died. The jury concluded that Frizer acted in self-defense, and he was pardoned. Marlowe's death is alleged by some to be an assassination, but the truth remains murky. Marlowe's short life was intertwined with the great themes of the age—the English Renaissance, religious conflict, and war between England and Spain. For someone like Marlowe it must have been an intoxicating mixture. As David Riggs says in his book *The World of Christopher Marlowe,* "Christopher Marlowe was an enigma, a pitiful mixture of brilliance and vice." The only portrait claimed to be of him hangs at Corpus Christi College in Cambridge. Beneath it are the words *Quod me nutrit me destruit,* which means *What feeds me destroys me.*

Are the people surrounding the Player's Plot real?

Edward Alleyn was a famous English actor who was born 1566 and died in 1626. He played the title roles in three of Christopher Marlowe's major plays: Faustus, Tamburlaine, and Barabas in *The Jew of Malta.*

Thomas Kyd was a playwright who was born in 1558 and died in 1594. He wrote *The Spanish Tragedy* in the 1580s—the play was also called *Hieronimo,* after the protagonist, and it was one of the most popular plays of the era. It is likely that Edward Alleyn played Hieronimo.

Philip Henslowe was a theatrical impresario who was born around 1550 and died in 1616. He produced a diary that is an interesting source of information about the theatrical world of the time. Henslowe had extensive business interests, including starch making, pawn broking, money lending, animal shows and bearbaiting, brothel keeping, but also running theaters. He established the Rose Theater in Bankside, South London, and commissioned and produced plays by Marlowe, Ben Jonson, and many other playwrights—although there is no record of him working with Shakespeare. He had a partnership with Edward Alleyn (who married his stepdaughter)—for example together they operated the Paris Gardens, a venue for bearbaitings south of the river—just as in *Day of Deliverance.*

Although there were many theatrical companies (the Admiral's Men, the Lord Chamberlain's men, etc.) the Henslowe Players are fictitious, as are the characters of Harry Fanshawe, Trinculo, Monk, and Christo, though Trinculo is a character in Shakespeare's play *The Tempest.* The Player's Plot is also fictitious, although acting troupes would frequently entertain at the royal palaces—including Hampton Court.

Who was Sir Francis Walsingham?

Sir Francis Walsingham was appointed Principal Secretary of State and Privy Councillor in 1573. He was born around 1532 and died in 1590. He developed the nation's first secret service, building up a network of more than a hundred secret agents across Europe. The operation penetrated Spanish military preparation and disrupted plots against the queen—including the Babington Plot, which resulted in the execution of Mary, Queen of Scots. Walsingham founded the theater company the Lord Chamberlain's Men—so his reward to the Henslowe Players in *Day of Deliverance* is quite true to life.

Day of Deliverance

Is Hampton Court real?
Yes. Hampton Court Palace is one of the most famous buildings in the United Kingdom and is situated next to the Thames near Kingston Upon Thames. The original Tudor palace was created by Cardinal Wolsey in around 1514, but when Wolsey fell from favor the palace was given to Henry VIII. The palace was expanded in the late seventeenth century by Christopher Wren for monarchs William and Mary—leaving the palace with two distinct architectural styles: Tudor and Baroque. The palace was the center of court and political life for nearly two hundred years and was built to host monarchs, their courtiers, and hundreds of servants. It has more than a thousand rooms and is set within stunning gardens and parks.

What was the English Renaissance?
The Renaissance was a cultural revolution that spread from Italy in the fourteenth and fifteenth centuries. It involved the rediscovery of Greek and Roman ideas and produced some of the finest art and architecture the world has ever seen. It was slow to spread to England. The fifteenth century in England was dominated by the Wars of the Roses, and Henry VIII's break with Rome in the 1520s discouraged connection with an artistic movement that focused on the Pope, the major sponsor of artists such as Michelangelo and Raphael. Also, Protestant opinion associated painting and sculpture with idolatry and so art was discouraged. This began to change in the late sixteenth century: a number of gifted painters sought asylum in England from Spanish persecution in the Netherlands; Henry's dissolution of the monasteries freed up land and materials, allowing property development; and Queen Elizabeth was herself enthusiastic about education—triggering interest in poetry, plays, and the theater. In architecture there were new "prodigy houses"—beautiful buildings like Hardwick Hall, Montacute, Longleat, Wollaton Hall, and Burghley House. In literature there was an explosion of creative energy—John Donne and Sir Philip Sidney in poetry, and Marlowe, Kyd, Jonson, and of course Shakespeare in theater. Song and dance also developed during Elizabeth's reign. Like her father, Henry VIII, Elizabeth was a talented

musician. A favorite dance of the queen's was the volta—where the man lifted his partner high in the air. The era produced many other famous figures—like Francis Bacon, who was a lawyer, politician, philosopher, scientist, and essayist.

The Taurus—Some Notes

The Taurus and its energy source stay put—in order to move through time and space, the traveler needs to have physical contact with a time phone. While back in time, the time phone is controlled and tracked by the Taurus using a set of codes. However, time travel is only possible when the Taurus has enough energy and when there is a strong enough carrier signal. As Jack and Angus have discovered, like the weather, the signal can be unpredictable and intermittent. The variability of the time signals is like shifting sands—periods of time open up and then close. Not all locations are accessible all the time. There is also deep time, which is a specific constraint meaning that the Taurus is only effective at transportation from when the traveler departs to more than about thirty years or so in the past. Anything sooner is a sort of no-go zone. This also means the traveler can't travel back from the past to just before he left. And finally there is the "Armageddon Scenario"—another part of time theory. It postulates that if you revisit the same point of space-time more than once, you dramatically increase the risk of a continuum meltdown. Space-time is like a bit of tissue paper, and moving within it is like putting holes in it with your finger. The tissue will hold together for a while, but too many holes and the whole thing will disintegrate. So you should not risk repeat trips in and around the same point. The precise parameters of this constraint are not known—and of course have not been tested.

ACKNOWLEDGMENTS

I would like to thank the following people for helping get Jack and Angus's adventures off the ground: Helen and Peter Flynn, Jamie Warren, Victoria Henderson, Caroline Knox, Pam Royds, Richard Scrivener, Amanda Wood, Ruth Huddleston, Phil Perry, Jayne Roscoe, Rachel Williams, Anne Finnis, Johnny Lambert, and Ruth Martin. I would also like to thank Stephen Alford (a real historian!) for input on Marlowe and King's College for *Day of Deliverance*. Most of all I would like to thank my wife, Sally, and children, Anna, Peter, and Tom, who have supported me throughout.